THE REALLY HIGH TEA

A SUB-INSPECTOR NAIR CAPER

BANGALORE CIVIL NUISANCE UNIT
BOOK ZERO

JOE CHACKO

This is a work of fiction.

Names, characters, places and incidents are either the product of the author's imagination or are used fictitiously.

Any resemblance to actual persons, living or dead, events or locales is coincidental.

Map image courtesy of Datawrapper

ISBN 9781838367336

 Created with Vellum

To my wife.
Without you: nothing.

Vasanth Nair's Cochin

Key locations in "The Really High Tea"

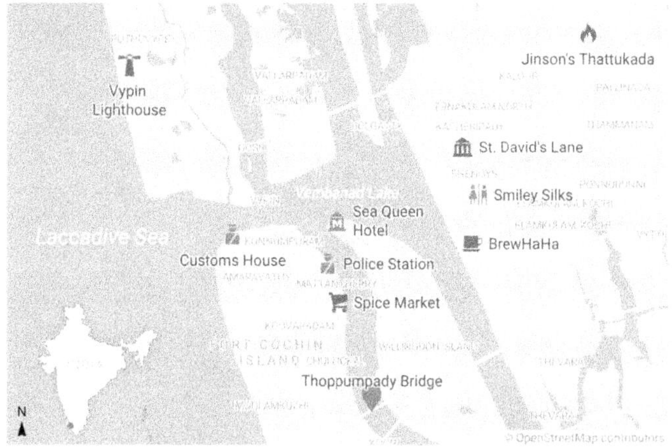

Map: Joe Chacko • Created with Datawrapper

I

There were many things that Sub-Inspector Vasanth Kamaraj Nair might have expected to see at 3.47pm on a Saturday afternoon in the Coconut Palm Lounge Restaurant at the Sea Queen Hotel on Cochin's Willingdon Point. None of those things included a portly matron, stripped down to her underclothes and undulating beside the hot buffet. Nair stopped in his tracks to take in the sight. Then wished he hadn't.

At the moment that he had received the call, Nair had been hard at work tailing a suspected smuggler through the maze of Jew Town's tiny streets. Jew Town was a teeming suburb in the north of Fort Cochin Island; the island was one of several that stood as a barrier between the incoming tidal flows of the Arabian Sea to the west and the town of Cochin a mile east on the mainland.

Nair's informant had assured him that the suspected smuggler would meet his paymaster that afternoon. The Sub-Inspector had stalked the man from the mosque to a run-down juice stall on the corner of a bustling street, a few hundred yards from the ramshackle jetty the fishermen offloaded at. Nair lurked in an adjacent alleyway, seeking solace from the sun in the finger-thin shadow cast by a telephone pole. He'd been mopping the sweat off his brow with his handkerchief when his phone buzzed.

It was Constable Kochukunju.

"Kochu!" Nair hissed, palming the phone. "I'm off-duty!"

"Sir!" It had seemed to be the only word Kochu could say. "Sir!"

"Oh, get on with it, idiot!"

"Sir," Kochu began again, "sir, you must come! There is a—problem!"

Nair glanced around the corner. His target was still there, sunglasses on, sipping watermelon juice through a straw and scrolling through his phone.

"Problem-shoblem!" Nair said. "Call Sub-Inspector Koshy, why don't you? He's on duty today, not me!"

Kochu gulped. "Sir, I tried, sir. But there is no answer. It went to voicemail. So I called you. You must come! It is a very, very big problem!"

Nair had attempted to clarify the nature of the 'very, very big problem', but Kochu's reply had been incoherent. The only words Nair had made out were "dancing" and "*ammachi*[1]" and "buffet". It had made no sense. Nair had been about to end the call with a suitably Shakespearean curse ("Away, you three-inch fool!") but, when he had looked out again, the target had vanished.

Nair raced out into the crossroads. His eyes scanned all points of the compass, while Constable Kochu babbled on. The streets teemed with pale, flabby, sleeveless foreigners, under pale, flabby hats, interspersed with ambling locals under sensible parasols. Jew Town was a warren of narrow alleyways and twisting lanes. The smuggler could have slipped into any of them. With a sinking heart, Nair realised that the cause was lost.

Nair padded back to where he had parked his vehicle. The moped wasn't a fitting vehicle for a dashing Sub-Inspector of Police—it did not inspire terror—but it had been cheap. Nair had little ready cash. His wealthy parents had not looked kindly on Nair's decision to leave the family business and join the police. Most purse strings had been severed; the single remaining one was fraying.

He had bought the moped second-hand from a retired college teacher; she'd thrown in the handbag carrier for free. He'd learned to live with that unwelcome embellishment and the garish cherry pink paintwork.

The moped possessed a meagre 50cc engine—it had been built for economy, not speed—but Nair found an injudicious twist of the throttle could set the thing going, provided one had fifty clear yards to begin with and no obstructions to brake for. Such auspicious circumstances were not to be found in bustling Jew Town that afternoon, but the Sub-Inspector achieved something similar by vigorous application of horn and much shouting.

The engine had howled as Nair raced south along the eastern flank of Fort Cochin island. At the Thoppumpady Bridge, he merged into the heavy traffic that rumbled over the strait. The moped's front wheel had barely touched the tarmac at Willingdon Island than Nair tilted the vehicle north, towards the Point at the very tip of the island.

It was a straight run up Indira Gandhi Road and Nair built up a head of steam. The wail of jet engines from the Naval Base to the right drowned out the engine's whining protest. On the left, the great waters of the strait kept Nair company, until they disappeared behind the squat, glistening cylinders of fuel tanks, the towers of the cement factory and the cranes of Mattancherry Wharf. Soon after, Nair saw the rows of drab government office blocks that heralded his destination, these looming over the moss-eaten edifices of ancient bungalows, now inhabited by ghosts and dust.

The Sea Queen Hotel lay at the very end of the road, sequestered from the surrounding shabbiness by spotless whitewashed walls and a manned gate. Nair, polo shirt soaked with sweat and straddling a woman's moped, looked dubious enough for the gate guard to flag him down.

"What's your business?" the beardless youth asked. The tone was insolent and there was nary a 'good afternoon' to be had. "Tradesmen's entrance is at the rear. That way. Front entrance is only for guests."

Nair fixed the man with a glare and extracted his ID from his trouser pocket. He stuck it in the man's face, taking some pleasure from the expected bloom of panic in the guard's eyes. The man ran to raise the barrier and even saluted as Nair zoomed past.

Even at pace, Nair could not help but wonder at the elegance of the landscaped grounds. The lawns were lush, the trees expertly pruned. There were topiary and marble sculptures of dancing elephants and reclining ladies. The azure blue of an infinity pool glinted at him from between the whitewashed walls of luxury bungalows.

Nair skidded to a stop on the hotel's gravel driveway. The Sea Queen's main entrance was a pale portico below a lime-washed tower block finished in the style of the *kottarams*[2] of Travancore[3] royalty. The eaves were edged with teak carvings. Marble balconies studded the walls. Orchids and flame lilies edged the paths, dancing in the breeze. Piano music filtered out from within. It all screamed exclusivity and luxury.

A pair of uniformed valets looked up from behind their station. They gave him an uncertain look.

Nair hauled the moped onto its stand. "Get over here!" he growled. "Police!"

One valet took a tentative step towards him. Nair threw the keys at him.

"Park it properly," Nair said, "or I'll park you when I come out!"

The man ran to obey. The other fled indoors. Nair followed in ill-temper.

The lobby was suitably sumptuous: acres of panelled wood, yards of soft furnishings, and ceiling lights glowing like a galaxy of subdued stars. There were more orchids, these arranged in bucket-sized artisan clay pots set on carved plinths at eye level, to fabulous effect.

The valet who had run in reappeared with a concierge at his shoulder. The concierge was twenty if a day and sported a short pompadour. His uniform, a cream-coloured quilted kurta pyjama[4], was spotless. The brass name badge on his breast said "JOMON".

"Cochin City Police," Nair said without preamble. "I'm Sub-Inspector Nair. I got a call. What's going on?"

The concierge elbowed the valet away, took a step forward, and bowed slightly. He gestured with an open hand across the lobby to a wood-framed arch at the other end. Through it, Nair caught a distant glimmer of the sea.

"This way, sir. In the Palm Lounge. Your colleague is there already. Permit me to show you." The concierge blinked. "It is simpler to show you than to explain."

As they trotted past the reception desk, Nair sucked his stomach in. He needn't have bothered—the two pretty young receptionists, immaculate in uniform cream saris, were so preoccupied by the shouting and crashing coming from beyond the arch that they did not notice Nair at all.

"What—," Nair said as they passed through. "Ah," he ended.

The Coconut Palm Lounge was open air, the elevated decking enclosed on all sides by waist-high carved rosewood panels. The roof above was traditional red clay tile, held up by ornate teak beams. Wooden columns framed the view onto the hotel grounds and beyond. The grounds contained more topiary, more sculptures, and several coconut palms swaying in the breeze. Beyond lay the great sweep of the ocean. The glimmer of the sun off the silvery filaments of Chinese fishing nets demarcated the coastline.

The restaurant was almost full, its tables set for the fabulous Saturday High Tea. Tabletops were polished to a high sheen. The silverware and glassware were spotless. The chafing dishes were piled high with intercontinental delicacies.

It should have been a sumptuous spectacle. The well-heeled patrons should have been stuffing their well-fed faces. The chefs in their whites should have been tending to the buffet. The waiting staff should have been flitting about bearing trays. The baby grand piano in the corner should have been emitting soothing melodies to whet the appetite. The air should have been full of the gentle tinkling of crushed ice in cocktail glasses.

All, though, was in abeyance and in silence. Some diners were on their feet, pointing. Others had their phones out, filming. Mothers clutched wriggling children close, napkins deployed as blindfolds. The chefs were all huddled in a corner, their ladles limp in their hands. The pianist cowered on his stool. All attention was on the dance floor.

The object of all attention was a large woman with silvery grey hair in a braid, who undulated in front of the piano. She was wearing only a blouse and underskirt. Her sari, yards of silk and sequins that cost more than Nair's moped, lay in loops and spirals that tracked her progress across the empty dance floor.

The matron's eyes were closed. The smile on her lips was rapturous. She raised her arms above her head. Her hips swung left, then right, then left again, in a furious machine-gun flurry. A beautifully dressed younger woman was at the matron's side, tugging gently at the lady's shoulders, but the dancer spun out of reach with an unexpected pirouette.

The dancer pointed at the pianist.

"Play!" she roared. "Play me a tune! Play!"

The pianist tugged at his bow tie and glanced over at the concierge in panic. Jomon waved back at him. The pianist nodded, straightened his tie and set to. He began *lento* but, in a few seconds, sped up to *allegro* as the matron gyrated towards him and clapped her hands to indicate her preferred tempo.

"Faster!" she cried. "Faster! Yes! Yes! That's it."

Nair rubbed his eyes and blinked. The vision was still there.

Now, three waiters sprinted out through the kitchen doors. Each bore a tablecloth stretched between his arms. They advanced on the dancer. In concert, they deployed themselves around the woman, their arms raised. The revolving array of starched fabric followed the aged dancer's uncertain orbit like satellites dedicated to the preservation of modesty.

Constable Kochu materialised at Nair's side, as dishevelled as ever in his uniform khaki. The constable was fifty-five years of age and had never progressed beyond the rank he had started at thirty years ago. His chief skill was extorting snacks from street vendors, as proven by his jowls and his paunch. Kochu offered Nair a half-hearted salute.

"Sir." Kochu said.

"What the bloody hell is this, Kochu?" Nair said, unable to take his eyes off the spectacle.

"I don't know, sir," Kochu said. "This was going on when I arrived."

Jomon, the concierge, broke in.

"Everything was normal, sir, until about forty-five minutes ago. Suddenly, this old lady got to her feet and began dancing. The restaurant manager, Mr. Thomas, called me immediately." Jomon shrugged. "He was concerned. So was I, but our philosophy is 'the customer is maharaja'. Or maharani, in this case. Everyone else seemed to enjoy it. Some customers were even clapping. So we did nothing. Until she began taking off her clothes. Then we called the police."

Nair stared at the concierge. Jomon shrugged and continued.

"The young lady there trying to get the old lady to sit down is her daughter-in-law. They both tried, she and her husband, the lady's son, but Madam was having none of it. She began shouting. Then the dancing got more energetic. It started as flamenco, I think. Stamping and clapping." Jomon tilted his head to peer through the gaps between the moving tablecloths. "Though now I think Madam has moved on to belly-dancing."

Kochu scratched his head under his hat. "What to do, sir? Should we arrest her?"

Nair pursed his lips. He hadn't joined the police to arrest old women. And while the old lady's state of undress was hardly decent, there was far more obscenity on public display on the cinema hoardings on Marine Drive, where scantily clad Bollywood actresses pouted at the world. An arrest seemed excessive, even to Nair.

"Where is the restaurant manager?" Nair said, treading water while his brain ticked over. "I need to speak to him. Bring him here. Now."

"He went to speak to the General Manager, sir," Jomon replied. "I'll go get him." The concierge ran off towards the lobby.

Nair turned to Kochu. "We'll have to restrain her at the least. Before she falls over and injures herself. Have you got your handcuffs?"

Kochu nodded and produced a pair.

"OK," Nair said. "Let's go. You go left, I'll go right." They took a step forward, then stopped.

Another player had entered the show now, his entry announced by a collective gasp from the horrified audience. A gaunt old man cantered on from stage left, arms flapping. His bald head shimmered under the lights. His dress shirt, a size too large, had pulled free from the waistband of his trousers; the shirt tails flapped as he skipped forward. The pensioner undid his belt as he advanced. He pulled it free and threw it to the floor with a flourish. His face split into a toothless grin—dentures, too, had been discarded.

"Aha!" shouted the old man. "Thancing! Leth's thance! Come on!" Clearly, consonants required teeth. "Gene Kelly!" he called to the crowd, "Thinging in tha rain!"

He began a ramshackle tap dance routine that started well, until the left foot failed to get out of the way of the right, and he ended up on his rear on the floor.

"Haha hahaha!" he laughed, all limbs skyward like an upturned beetle. With an energy unseen in geriatrics, the man kicked out with one leg and spun around on his back. "Breakthance! Breakthance!"

"Bloody hell!" Nair said. "Quick, Kochu! Before he dislocates a hip! How many handcuffs do you have?"

Kochu looked crestfallen. "Um, only one pair, sir. I didn't expect—"

Nair set his jaw. "Right," he said. "We'll have to improvise. You call for backup. And more handcuffs. Once you've done that, round up a few waiters and tackle the breakdancer. I'm going in for the belly dance."

2

By the time Sub-Inspector Jimmy Koshy trotted into the Coconut Palm Lounge twenty-eight minutes later, Nair had restored order. The restaurant had been emptied, the patrons sequestered on the manicured lawn outside. The guests huddled under the shade offered by the coconut palms, each cluster attended by a single, sweating police constable bearing a notepad. Waiters darted over the grass with trays bearing tall, frosted glasses, the complimentary drinks having been assembled en masse and with some haste by the duty bartenders.

Within the restaurant, it was a flurry of activity. More waiters rushed between tables, clearing plates bearing half-eaten meals. Music rose above the clanking of crockery. The pianist, restored to his position, played renditions of old Bollywood hits with intense focus. The only spot of stillness was the single table nearest the buffet where lounged Sub-Inspector Vasanth Nair. A gaggle of chefs bearing plates of food surrounded him. Nair was chewing.

"And what is that?" Nair asked, in between swallows. He pointed his fork at a plate.

"Chicken Bunny Chow, sir," said the head chef, a grave man with a salt-and-pepper moustache and a gourmand's full cheeks. The head chef bowed slightly and presented the plate for inspection. "It is a very traditional South African street food. From the city of Durban, in fact, where there are many Indian migrants. This is a bread loaf filled with chicken curry and vegetables. Very delicious. May I serve you some?"

"God! No!" Nair replied. Nair's fork pointed at the head chef. "I am vegetarian! I don't eat chicken. Especially served with bunnies! Away with that! Get me something else."

"Certainly, sir," the head chef said. He thrust the plate at a sous chef, who ran off with it. "While Sir is waiting for the next course, perhaps Sir would like to sample another mocktail?"

"Mmm," Nair said, taking a sip. "Yes. Another one of these. What is this drink called?"

"That is 'Kiss of the Sun'. Watermelon, papaya, orange. And honey. 100% vegetarian."

Nair nodded. Another sous chef ran off, almost colliding with Koshy.

"O-ho!" Nair's voice rose. "The much lamented Sub-Inspector Koshy. Hell is empty and all the devils are here."

"What the hell are you talking about, Nair?" Koshy said in a growl.

Nair grinned back at him. "That's Shakespeare, my dear fellow. The Tempest. Which is what this place was before you arrived. But never fear. I have restored calm. No need to thank me." Nair used a foot to shove a chair across the floor towards Koshy. "Sit. Have a bite to eat. The constables are interviewing the witnesses. There are at least thirty. Witnesses, that is. Only four constables, but it's the week-end. That's all we could rustle up at short notice."

With little grace, Koshy dragged the chair back to the table and sat. Koshy placed his elbows on the tablecloth and leaned forward.

"Nair-" he began.

Nair raised the fork at him. "A moment." The fork swivelled towards the culinary assembly. "Away, fellows. Sub-Inspector Koshy and I need to have a chat. Oh, and return with some of those spring rolls. The vegetarian ones. Freshly fried, mind. Not cold and old."

Audience dispersed, Nair turned to the glowering Koshy. "You were saying?"

Koshy looked fit to be tied. "I was asking what the hell is going on here!"

Nair took another sip of his mocktail. "I'll get to that. First, where were you? You're on duty today. What exactly were you doing that Kochu could not raise you?" Nair's brow furrowed. He leaned towards Koshy and sniffed the air. "And why do you smell of bananas? *Ethakkappam*[1], to be precise. Were you stuffing your face, Koshy? Was that it? You should know better, what with your body mass index and waist circumference. You're on the road to diabetes, Koshy."

Koshy sucked his stomach in. "None of your business. I'm here now. What's going on?"

"Ha. Wouldn't you like to know? Maybe I'll tell you. Or maybe I won't. Maybe, when Inspector Kurien rings you for an update, I'll let you gasp for a while, like a landed mackerel."

Koshy chewed on a lip. "Nair. Listen. I was engaged in important official work. I will tell you about it later. Right now, I need to know what's going on here in case Inspector Kurien hears of it. And yes, I'm sorry I didn't materialise the instant I was called. But I'm here now. So stop being an ass and fill me in!"

The timely arrival of more mocktails and a platter of steaming spring rolls interrupted Nair's retort. By the time the two Sub-Inspectors had consumed three spring rolls apiece, the mood had improved.

"Fine," Nair said. "Fine. But you owe me, Koshy. Never forget that."

Koshy dunked his spring roll in the chilli dipping sauce with a vigour that suggested he would rather stick it in Nair's eye.

"Alright," Koshy grunted. He took a bite. "OK. I owe you one."

By the time Nair had finished his tale, the spring rolls were all gone, all except for the one on Koshy's fork, suspended halfway to Koshy's open mouth.

"Are you seriously suggesting," Koshy said, "that two geriatrics sprang into break-dancing and belly-dancing in the middle of the buffet? It's complete nonsense." He swivelled in his chair and scanned the room. "Where are they now?"

"Quarantined," Nair replied. "Once we'd snared them with tablecloths, they calmed down. I sent them upstairs. With a family member apiece. The manager found some empty rooms. They should each be under a duvet. The victims, not the family member. Door closed. Lights off. Curtains drawn. We've summoned the hotel doctor to check on them." The fork pointed. "Are you going to eat that before it gets cold?"

Koshy stuck the spring roll in his mouth. He considered the matter as he chewed. He swallowed.

"What do you think caused it?" Koshy said. "Were the victims related?"

"No," Nair replied. "Different family groups. And they arrived at different times. No connection, so far as I can tell, apart from being rich enough to afford 1950 rupees per head for lunch. That's before tax, by the way. And drinks. Neither geriatric consumed alcohol, though there was alcohol at the table. Both drank mocktails. I suspected the food, so I began an analysis of their plates. I've been working my way through the suspect foodstuffs. For the sake of forensics. And justice. The vegetarian stuff only, of course." Nair patted his stomach. "It's not the food, though. I feel fine. And all the other customers are fine. This is a buffet. They've all been stuffing their faces, the gluttons. If all the food was contaminated, this place would look like a psychedelic discotheque."

"You say the two victims went gaga within, what, half an hour of each other?"

Nair nodded. "Exactly." He brushed the crumbs off his shirt. "Regardless of what caused it, there's no crime here. Bit of a commotion, sure, but I don't think the hotel will be interested in a prosecution for public indecency. This is not very public. And it wasn't all that indecent, just unappetising."

Nair drained his drink in one go, then got to his feet.

"Ah!" he said, setting the glass down. "I recommend the Kiss of the Sun. Superb. And ask the chefs if you're still hungry. They'll get you whatever you want." Nair consulted his notebook. "In fact, I'd suggest you try the chicken lababdar and the Malabar Club Sandwich. Those are still untested. And the Black Forest Gateau. Both victims had the Black Forest. That could be the link." Nair paused for a moment. "On second thoughts, maybe let Kochu do the rest of the eating. Can't have the senior officer on the scene break into break-dancing in full view of the general public."

Koshy shot to his feet. "Where are you going? I thought—"

"You thought nothing, Koshy, old chap," Nair said. "I'm on my day off. I'm going home for a nap. This is your show now. Good luck."

"But, but, Nair-"

"No but-buts, Koshy. You're on duty. You deal with it. I'm off. Farewell."

Nair turned towards the doorway, then stopped. Concierge Jomon was rushing towards them, arms flapping. Jomon waved furiously at them.

"Sir! Sir! You have to come! Please! In the lobby!"

Nair broke into a trot, Koshy at his shoulder. "Bloody hell. What is it? What's wrong now?"

Jomon sprinted back towards the lobby. He shouted over his shoulder.

"It's the manager, sir! Mister Thomas! He's—he's dancing!"

They slid to an untidy halt just short of the reception desk. When Nair had last seen him, Manager Thomas had been neat and dignified, if a little anxious, at what had erupted in his restaurant. Thomas had been the model of efficiency, giving Nair a concise account and following Nair's instructions to the letter. Nair had been impressed with the man.

Now, Manager Thomas was prancing about on top of the reception desk, legs akimbo, arms raised. He had flung his uniform jacket to the floor. His necktie was wrapped around his head. The two female receptionists were hugging each other in the far corner, eyes wide with horror. The other concierge was plucking gently at the manager's trouser cuffs, his voice pleading with Thomas to "come down, sir! Please come down!"

Nair realised that Manager Thomas was doing a passable impression of a *Kathakali*[2] dancer. The manager's shoulders rose and fell, marking time.

"Thak-a-thaaa. Thak-a-thaa," sang the manager, his voice emulating the syncopated drums that would normally accompany such a recital. "Thak-a-thaa. Thak-a-thaaaaa!" His head swivelled this way and that, eyes darting from side to side. "I am Arjuna[3]! I am a warrior! See me and fear!"

Manager Thomas glanced down at the concierge. "Release me, fool!" he cried. He kicked at the concierge, and connected. The concierge spun to the floor, landing with a thump.

Nair unbuttoned his top button. Eyes fixed on the manager, he called out to Koshy.

"Koshy. Take Jomon. Get the equipment."

Koshy turned, then stopped. His usually deep voice was high and thin. "What equipment? What should I get?"

"Tablecloths." Nair said. He'd slipped his shoes off. Nair put one foot on the reception desk and hauled himself up. "Four. At least four."

Manager Thomas proved to be far more of a challenge than the other two. For one, he was younger. He had also clearly had some classical dance training—the *mudras*[4] he made were almost martial. Despite their best efforts, no one could get close without the risk of losing an eye. In the end, Nair ordered the concierges to fetch a mattress ("king size, mind!"). When they had laid that in place, it was a simple matter to knock the manager off onto it and swathe him with waiting tablecloths.

"Interesting," Koshy said from a safe distance, as the bell boys dragged the mattress away. "You're right, Nair.

The moment he's covered up, he calms down. Just some quiet babbling."

Nair was mopping his brow with a hot lavender-scented towel that Jomon had presented to him on a tray.

"Always late to the party, Koshy. I told you that already. Now, I'm leaving." Nair pointed at the concierge. "Jomon, fetch my vehicle."

Koshy joined Nair on the driveway.

"Listen, Nair," Koshy said, "I might need a hand with this one. As I said earlier, I've got something else on, so if you could see your way to helping me out, I'd owe you one."

"You already owe me one, Koshy. Or have you forgotten? That makes two."

Koshy grimaced. "Alright, fair enough. I'll owe you two. In fact, I'll make it three. Fair? What do you say?"

Before Nair could answer, the concierge arrived on the moped. Jomon braked too hard—the vehicle wobbled as the tires skidded on the gravel.

"Careful! Careful!" Nair shouted. "It's not a bloody Ferrari! Get off!"

Nair let Koshy stew while he mounted the moped.

"Fine," Nair said. "I'll cover if needs be. And you'll owe me. But you deal with the rest of this today. And no griping when I ask for payback. Clear?"

Koshy's face lit up with relief. "Fine. Great. No problem."

Nair revved the engine and was just about to set off when fresh shouting assailed them.

From above.

They looked skywards.

There was a man on the balcony two storeys up. The man was naked apart from a pair of mustard yellow boxer shorts. And he was dancing. It could have been hip-hop. Or Bharatnatyam[5]. It was hard to tell from a distance.

"Oh, for heaven's sake!" Koshy said. "Not another one." He threw Nair a pleading look. "Nair—"

"No!" Nair said. He put the moped into first gear. "Absolutely not. Three favours is three more than usual for a Saturday. This is all yours. You know what to do. I'll see you tomorrow at the station for the debrief."

With that, Nair released the clutch and rattled off through the palms.

3

The next morning, Inspector Anil Kurien alighted from the auto-rickshaw outside the gates of the Cochin Women & Children's Hospital. Kurien was in a foul mood. The auto-driver, sensing it, did not wait for payment, nor did Kurien offer. The police did not pay. That was the natural order of things.

It was Sunday. Sunday was not, in Kurien's book, a day when an Inspector of Police should have to attend to duties. That was what junior officers were for. That, too, was the natural order of things.

And yet, here he was. On a Sunday. Attending to duties. Most unnatural. Most unsatisfactory.

Preserving the natural order of things had been Inspector Kurien's chief aim throughout his long career. It helped that Kurien had married well—his wife's uncle was a Member of the Legislative Assembly[1]. With the right inducements, Uncle Cherian had ensured that Kurien's police postings had been in tranquil, rural locations, where Kurien could concentrate on preserving himself, encountering none of the hazards associated with the prosecution of justice. Kurien had spent ten years in Idukki District, a forested plateau snuggled between the hills of the Western Ghats. The key local industries were tea-growing and nature tourism, neither of which generated much crime. Which was just how Kurien liked it.

This happy state of affairs might have persisted until Kurien retired, but the last parliamentary elections had seen Uncle Cherian's party booted out of power. Uncle Cherian could not escape the consequences. Nor could Uncle Cherian's protégés.

"It will be fine, Kurien," Uncle Cherian had said. Cherian had been washing his hands after a lavish lunch at Kurien's spacious police quarters in Idukki. The election results had just been announced and Uncle Cherian had lost his seat. To mark the end of his tenure, Cherian had conducted a whistle-stop tour of his beneficiaries to collect his dues. Though Idukki was out of the way, lunch at his nephew-in-law's had been on the itinerary. Kurien's wife had gone to town on the menu: chicken biryani, fried fish, fish curry, beef curry, beef fry, chicken fry, sambar, rasam, raita, poppadums and three kinds of pickle. Cherian had tucked in without comment, as if such a meal were an everyday happening. Which, Kurien supposed, it was for a politician.

"It will be fine," Cherian said again. "You're being posted to Mattancherry. In Cochin. I couldn't wangle anything easier. Cochin is very different from this place, but a resourceful man should be able to make the most of it. Anyway, you only have two more years to serve. Just keep your head down and it will be over soon. I know the current Inspector there. A sound man. I'll have a word with him, just to make sure he eases you in when you arrive."

Kurien had expressed his thanks with four bottles of

single-malt Scotch and a bar of gold bullion that he had bought at great expense from a local smuggler, who had acquired it, at a lesser expense, from an associate in Dubai.

It hadn't taken Kurien long to settle into his new post. Though the city of Cochin was a far cry from the gentle hills of Idukki, and though there was a lot of actual work, there were also opportunities to capitalise on. With his predecessor's help, and with the judicious deployment of further incentives, Kurien slotted in neatly.

The natural order had been re-established, until, with barely months to go before his retirement, the Commissioner had saddled Kurien with two young Sub-Inspectors, these a pair of rascals that now threatened to bring Kurien's carefully constructed edifice crashing down.

Kurien set his hat on his head and strode across the tiny junction towards the gates of Mattancherry Police Station, always open and perpetually lopsided. The rendered boundary walls were grey and mouldy, the appearance unimproved despite Sub-Inspector Nair's recent innovation of potted plants set atop. It was like gilding a turd, Kurien thought, but he had found no reason to oppose it. No one had stolen any of the pots, which pleased Kurien—it would have been bad for his reputation if they had, and he would have had to do something about it.

There was the usual throng of civilians at the gates, much the same as at the hospital across the road. Misfortune and circumstance continued to operate on Sundays. The civilians leapt aside as Kurien approached. A few wished him 'good morning', which he dismissed with a 'hmph', again part of the natural order. In his view, power was best expressed in the withholding of common courtesy to those of no consequence.

Kurien ignored the guard's salute and strode through

the doors. The reception desk was unmanned, as were all the other desks in the open-plan office behind. The ceiling fans spun slowly, redistributing the torpid air. His nostrils detected a faint aroma of food. He looked at his watch. It was only ten o'clock—far too early for lunch.

The distant sound of voices guided his steps. It was a conversation, he realised, a heated one. Coming from the office that the two Sub-Inspectors shared.

Kurien gritted his teeth. It was those two idiots that caused all this. He was sure of it.

Of the two recruits, Sub-Inspector Jimmy Koshy had been the easier to get the measure of. He had pocketed, without demur, the brown envelope that Kurien deposited in Koshy's desk drawer every month. In turn, Kurien did not question Koshy's liberal personal use of impounded motor vehicles. After all, Kurien thought, Koshy paid for the petrol for the Bullet[2] out of his own pocket—it was better the thing be ridden rather than rot away in the vehicle pound until they auctioned it off. Kurien and Koshy reached an unspoken understanding.

Sub-Inspector Vasanth Nair was an altogether different proposition. Nair's brown envelope reappeared in Kurien's desk drawer the morning after the monthly distribution. Nair was vigorous in his enforcement of the law, leading to turbulence in the placid waters of commerce in Mattancherry. Nary a day passed without Nair arresting some employee of one of Kurien's associates. On trivial issues. Drunkenness. Gambling. Fighting. Rudeness.

Kurien's associates were up in arms. Some had even reduced their monthly tributes. More threatened to do so. Sub-Inspector Nair was a genuine threat to the natural order, but one that Kurien could not see off. Perhaps this would be the opportunity.

Treading softly, Kurien slipped through the doorway.

A row of backs greeted him. Four constables stood before the two desks in the room. Vasanth Nair stood behind his desk, hands on hips, staring to his left at Sub-Inspector Koshy, who lounged in his own chair behind his own desk.

"Well," Nair said, "am I right? Admit I'm right, Koshy. Stop being so pig-headed."

Kurien cleared his throat. Heads turned. The row of backs dissipated as the constables leapt out of the way.

Nair saluted. An instant later, Koshy leapt to his feet and did the same.

Kurien gave Nair a cutting look. "What the hell is going on here?" Kurien could not believe his eyes. Crockery covered the surface of Nair's desk. There were plates and teapots and cafetières and crystal glasses. "What is this? A bloody tea party?"

"No, sir," Nair said. "It's evidence."

"Evidence? What evidence? And what are you doing here, Nair? Koshy's on duty this weekend." Kurien turned his baleful gaze on the other officer. "Start talking, Koshy. Make it quick."

Koshy gulped. He took a breath before laying out, at breakneck speed, the events that had taken place at the Sea Queen Hotel the day before. "We—I think it's something to do with the food, sir," Koshy said. "That's what all that is. Evidence."

Nair read from his notebook. "Specifically, three servings of Black Forest cake, two plates of chicken lababdar, two palak paneers, two cocktails, two mocktails. And tea. Four pots of tea." Nair flipped his notebook closed. "It's the tea. I'm sure of it."

Koshy snorted. “Nonsense. It could be anything. How do you know—”

“Enough!” Kurien shouted. He pointed at the constables. “All of you! Out! Back to your desks!”

Once the room had emptied, Kurien turned to his junior officers. Kurien fished his mobile phone out and held it up to the officers. “Do you see this? Go on. Have a look.”

Koshy stood rooted to the spot. It was Nair who leant forward and took the phone from Kurien’s hand.

“Ah. Yes. A video.” Nair said. “That’s the belly-dancing granny. Oh, and here comes the break-dancer.” He looked up at Kurien. “Sir. How did you get this?”

“YouTube.” Kurien said in a whisper. His voice grew in volume as he went on. “On bloody YouTube! This is what I was rung about. This morning. At breakfast. By the Deputy Inspector General of Police. On a Sunday morning. The DIG, did you hear me? While I was halfway through my appam[3].”

“Ah,” said Nair.

Kurien took a step forward. “Ah. Ah, you say? Funny, that, because ‘Ah’ is what I said to the DIG. ‘Ah’. Do you want to know what the DIG said then? Do you?”

Nair shook his head.

“I’ll tell you,” Kurien said, advancing. “He said ‘Why is there a video of the ruling party’s Deputy Leader’s grandfather breakdancing on YouTube, Kurien?’ That’s what he said. And do you know what I said?”

“That you don’t know?” Nair offered.

“Yes!” Kurien roared. “Yes! That is exactly what I said. To which the DIG said, ‘Well, you’d better bloody well find out, Kurien. Because the Deputy Leader is not happy. So, I’ve written a transfer order. With your name on it. For a police outpost in the jungle. The signature goes on it this evening. Unless I hear from you before then.'"

"Ah," Nair said. He tried a smile. "Well, now you know."

The entry of Constable Kochu aborted Inspector Kurien's next outburst. A slender man in chef's whites accompanied the constable.

Kurien spun around to take them in. "And who the hell is this now?"

The civilian gave the officers a small bow. "Anand Bora, sirs. I am the Tea Master at the Sea Queen." Bora was barely five feet tall and of Assamese[4] heritage.

Koshy spoke up. "Tea Master? Kochu, I told you to bring the Food & Beverage manager."

Bora bowed again. "My boss sends his apologies, sir. When he heard what the matter was, he sent me. I was on duty yesterday when it happened. He was not. Perhaps I can help?"

Nair looked at Kurien. "With your permission, sir. The tea is the only common factor. There were four victims: the old lady, the old man, the manager and the upstairs guest. They all had tea. In those four pots. I'm sure it was the tea that did it."

All eyes were on Kurien. The Inspector took a deep breath, then exhaled loudly.

"Fine. Do it." He glared at Nair, then Koshy. "You'd better hope it is the tea, gentlemen. Or the Black Forest. Or the chicken. Because if it's not, there are going to be two more names for the DIG to add to his transfer order."

4

The policemen gathered around the desk as Tea Master Bora began his inspection. Bora rearranged the items on the desktop so that the four teapots stood in a line. All four were identical, perfect glazed white bone china with a gold inlay of palm leaves. Bora removed the lids and placed them to one side.

"These are definitely our teapots," Bora said, to no response. "First, let me assess the fragrance." He bent forward from the waist and sniffed at the teapots. When he stood upright again, he looked puzzled.

"Well?" Kurien said.

Bora turned to him. "It doesn't smell quite right, sir. All four smell odd. I must taste." From the breast pocket of his chef's tunic, Bora took out a silver spoon with an elongated handle. "My personal tasting spoon, sir. Australian. Best quality. The implement should not taint the taste." He did not see Kurien roll his eyes.

Bora dipped the spoon into the first pot, then tasted. Bora's face screwed up. He reached for a half-empty mock-tail glass and spat into it.

Bora shook his head. "That's not right. There is a taint. Very subtle, but distinctive."

Nair couldn't contain himself. "What—"

Bora held up a hand. "Please, sir. I must taste the other three samples. I beg your patience. Tasting should not be rushed."

The police officers waited, with poor grace. Kurien tapped a foot. Koshy scratched. Nair smoothed his moustache. Finally, Bora wiped the spoon dry, tucked it back into his pocket, and turned to them.

"Yes," Bora said. "There is a taint. One moment." He reached into his trouser pocket and retrieved a sheaf of receipts. He flicked through them quickly. "These are the point-of-sale receipts for the victims, sorry, guests. Yes. It is as I thought." Bora looked up at them. "All four ordered tea."

Nair snapped. "Oh, for heaven's sake, we know that, man. The question is, was it the tea that did it?"

Bora nodded. "Perhaps. They all ordered tea. In fact, they all ordered our special blend. It is on promotion. Russian Caravan." He pointed at the teapots. "This is definitely Russian Caravan. It has the malt flavour of Assam tea and the smokiness of Fujian Lapsang. Also, a hint of Nepalese leaf, as per our specification. But—"

"But?" Kurien said. "But what?"

Bora looked puzzled. "There is a bitterness to it that should not be there. It might be impossible for an untrained person to detect, but, to me, it is obvious." He looked from one policeman to the other. "The tea is tainted. I am sure of it."

Kurien turned to Constable Kochu. "Take a statement from this fellow," Kurien said, pointing at Bora. "Do it properly. Even the spelling, Kochu. The DIG will be reading it."

Fear bloomed in Kochu's eyes. He saluted, then retreated with Bora in tow. Kurien turned back to his Sub-Inspectors.

"Well? What do we do now? Koshy! Speak up!"

Koshy had settled onto his desk. He shot to his feet.

"Well, sir, I think, maybe, we should possibly, um, investigate the hotel?" Kurien's frown grew darker. Koshy sped up. "On second thoughts, maybe we should hand it over to Public Health? Food contamination. Not a police matter. I think. That way, we won't have to investigate." Koshy watched carefully, hoping his reply had found favour.

Kurien shook his head. "Fine idea. Except it's too late. The DIG is now involved. Which means we're involved." He sighed. "There's no escape. We'll have to investigate. It was a good idea, though. Very good. You'll make a fine Inspector. When the time comes." Kurien's eyes narrowed. "If you survive."

Nair's voice rang out. "We should quarantine the remaining tea. At the hotel. And send these teapots to the forensics lab. For toxicology analysis. That's the logical next step."

Kurien crossed his arms and glared at Nair. "Hmph. Always leaping forward, isn't it, Sub-Inspector Nair? Too much leaping leads to falling over." Kurien turned his head away and addressed Koshy. "See to it, Koshy. You're in charge of this case. Nair will look after all other affairs at the station while you give this priority. Wrap it up quickly. Understand? Good. I'm off to call the DIG."

Kurien stopped on the threshold to cast a final warning over his shoulder. "Make sure you don't give the DIG any further reason to call me. Understood?"

Nair crashed back into his chair, setting the crockery rattling. Koshy perched back down on the end of his desk.

"Well," Nair said, arms crossed. "You should be thrilled. You're in charge. Of a case the DIG has an interest in. Lucky you." There was a trace of bitterness in Nair's voice. "A chance to make a name for yourself, Koshy."

Koshy chewed at a lip, then shook his head.

"It's not so simple, Nair. As I told you, I've got something else on. Something far more important than this tea nonsense. A proper crime. It's all going to go down in the next few days. I can't be shuttling back and forth to Willingdon Island four times a day to examine teapots." Koshy looked Nair in the eye. "You said you'd cover for me, Nair."

Nair shook his head. "I've done enough for you, you ingrate. I'm just going to settle in here for a week or two, lick my wounds and do paperwork."

Koshy got to his feet. He placed both hands on Nair's desk and leaned forward so his face was only a foot away from Nair's.

"Look at you," Koshy said, grinning. "You're champing at the bit. You're raring to go. And why not? It was you who cracked the tea mystery. You're the one who knew what to do on the scene. This case is rightfully yours, Nair. It's just that Kurien doesn't trust you. Or like you. And you know why."

Nair said nothing, simply looked out through the bars in the open window.

"Listen," Koshy said, "Mattancherry is a dead-end. There's no advancement here. Kurien just wants a quiet life until he retires. And his replacement will be some other idle clown. We both know that. What I'm working on might get me out of here. And, if you help me, I might swing something for you. Special Branch, maybe. Or Drugs Squad.

Maybe even the Armed Police Division." Koshy leaned in further. "Imagine that, Nair. There'd be rifles. Body armour. Mobs. Riots. You'd love it."

There was the merest twitch of a Nair eyebrow before Nair spoke.

"What is this case you're working on, Koshy? Spill the beans."

Koshy shook his head. "It's top secret. But it's big. I'll tell you when I can. Promise. So, what do you say? Is it a deal?"

Nair smoothed his moustache with forefinger and thumb. "Very well. Okay. It's a deal. I'll investigate the High Tea case for you. But who covers the station?"

Koshy let out a sigh of relief. "Great. Bugger the station. Kochu can run it. That's how it usually works. I mean, Kurien's hardly here. So long as you and I pop our heads in now and then, Kurien won't know any different. Leave it to me. I'll have a word with Kochu and arrange a proper 'incentive' for his participation."

Koshy fished his motorcycle keys out of his pocket. "Right. I'm off. I'm supposed to be doing surveillance this—erm, forget I said that. Good luck on the case. And ring me if you need anything." Koshy headed for the door. Nair called after him.

"Koshy—"

Koshy replied without breaking stride. "Yes, Nair. I owe you four."

5

Jaykishan Nambiar had reason to be pleased with his achievements to date. The predictions of his schoolteachers had been dire—and almost proven true. Nambiar had barely passed his SSLC[1] examinations. He had failed the national university entry test for medicine and engineering. At age twenty-eight, he was unmarried. But Nambiar had ploughed his own furrow. And made a go of it.

Starting Cochin's first ever "luxury beverage boutique" had seemed a laughable idea years ago. Many had laughed at it to his face. However, Jaykishan Nambiar (or '@JKN' as he styled himself on Instagram) had foreseen the economic wave building, and had poised himself to ride it.

Nambiar realised early on that it was aspiration that fuelled human desire. There was no point flogging cheap bargains to the masses. No, the way in was to go large. There was always a market for luxury. With the relaxation of India's fiscal rules, that market grew beyond measure. Nambiar exploited it and flourished while his peers struggled to stay afloat under the weight of their 'respectable' jobs and 'respectable' marriages.

Nambiar's expensive private education had finally come in handy. He had learnt little in the classroom but he had moved in the orbit of similarly disinterested youth, sons of affluent businessmen, those with ready access to 'black money[2]' that needed to be laundered. It had only taken a few words in the right ears, three meetings and a handful of handshakes to see his dream come to fruition.

Money alone could not have positioned his business in the heart of 'on trend' Marine Drive. Nambiar could not have secured the expensive lease without the exercise of his patrons' influence. The bungalow his premises were located in had been built by the Dutch in the 1800s. The Kerala Art Academy had put in a bid to the Municipal Corporation to house an art gallery in it however, thanks to more words in more ears, Nambiar had secured a ninety-nine-year lease on the ground floor, and BrewHaHa had come into being.

There was no shortage of custom. The art gallery upstairs attracted the literati. And Instagram brought in the affluent college students who attended nearby St. Veronica's Academy. Where the rich and the beautiful went, the rest of the world followed. Tourists were, of course, as perennial as moths, drawn to the ambience of the waterfront as seen from BrewHaHa's Courtyard Garden Cafe. At sunset, the brilliant red flowers of the Flame of the Forest trees along the promenade framed the glowing lights of distant islands and passing ferries in a style that begged to be digitised, hashtagged and Liked on social media.

Nambiar had been an awkward child, but in his new avatar as @JKN, he embraced the role of successful young entrepreneur and social media darling. He learned how to keep his customers happy. For most, that meant fawning over them, making them feel special, a selfie here, a selfie there. Occasionally, though, he had to deal with oddballs, people who really didn't belong, who really didn't have the money but who wished to inhabit the same space as the movers and shakers. These he gave some time and a little effort, but grudgingly.

This oddball had already taken far too much of both. The man had settled himself at a courtyard table and perused the menu for far too long. He had ordered nothing, dismissing the waiter with the statement that he was 'waiting for someone'. After half an hour, the waiter had informed the manager, who approached the man himself. This time, the man had ordered an iced tea, remarking at the 'eye-watering prices'. After another half-hour of nursing his drink, the man was still there, which is when the manager had found Nambiar.

Nambiar eyed the man from the sanctuary of the pass. The customer was tall and well-groomed, but clearly not of BrewHaHa's usual clientele. His checked shirt was cotton, as were his unbranded khaki slacks. The shoes were black leather lace-ups, not Converse. And he spoke in Malayalam, not English, the accent very much that of South Kerala. It was all highly unsatisfactory. The bright, young things inhabiting the other tables were too wrapped up in their bright, young chatter to notice or care, but Nambiar noticed. And cared.

"I'll deal with him," Nambiar said to the manager. He grabbed a menu and made his way to the table. The man glanced up as Nambiar positioned himself. The customer had a rather fine nose and a well-manicured moustache in the style of ageing Malayalam film heroes.

"Would you care to see the menu, sir?" Nambiar asked,

with a tight smile. He placed the menu on the table. "Our special today is grilled chicken Caesar salad."

The man shook his head. "No. I'm vegetarian."

"Oh. Well, we also have banana bread French toast, cheese tart, fish and chips." Nambiar paused. "We could just bring you chips—if you're on a budget. And our roasted vegetable wrap is very, um, affordable. It's served with a tahini yoghurt sauce."

The man glared at Nambiar. "And you are?"

"The owner. Jaykishan is my name, but my friends call me JKN."

The man blinked. "JKN? Isn't that the airport code for Jakarta? You don't look Indonesian."

Nambiar bristled. It was time for hard tacks. "Sir, if you're not going to order anything else—"

The man waved him to silence. "I'm looking for a particular blend of tea. I was told this was the premier tea boutique in all of Cochin." He pointed at the menu. "Yet, I see you don't have it listed on your menu. Quite disappointing."

Nambiar was taken aback. "Oh? Which blend was it?"

"Russian Caravan. I sampled some at the Sea Queen last weekend. At the Saturday High Tea. Most interesting. Sensational, some might say. When I enquired, they said that your firm provided this blend."

"Ah. Yes. That is an extra-premium blend we produce only for the Sea Queen. One of five such unique blends that the hotel commissioned especially. Unfortunately, we don't offer that for sale. It's part of our exclusivity agreement. Perhaps—"

The man got to his feet. His gaze was elsewhere. Nambiar turned to see what had attracted his attention.

Through the open gate leading from the courtyard to

the street, Nambiar saw a police jeep pull up. The driver got out, followed by another police officer. This second was rather short, old, and plump. They made their way through the gates, heading straight for Nambiar.

Nambiar turned to face them, forgetting the tea fancier entirely. He was aware of his heartbeat thumping in his ears. He stood rooted to the spot as the policemen approached. The short one seemed to hold a blue metal tin in his hands. A familiar blue metal tin.

"Sir." The short policeman tucked the tin under his left arm and saluted with the right. Nambiar was wondering whether to return the salute when the tea fancier spoke.

"About time, Kochu. I expected you half an hour ago."

Kochu grinned. "Traffic, sir. Terrible over the bridge."

Nambiar turned back to his customer. Sub-Inspector Nair fixed him with a beady eye.

"Right, you. I'm Sub-Inspector Vasanth Nair. Mattancherry Police. We can discuss this out here, or in your office. Your choice."

All the conversation in the courtyard had stopped. Everyone was watching the scene unfold in front of them. Nambiar knew the phones would be out next. It would be all over Instagram in a minute.

"Please," Nambiar said. "Let's go inside. To my office. This way."

Nambiar's office was quite the most luxurious work-space Vasanth Nair had visited in a professional capacity. The wooden office furniture was carved from rosewood, the floor was polished marble, and the desktop computer was a glistening chrome cube with a matching oversized screen. A single pane of tinted glass occupied the entire wall behind Nambiar's desk, looking out onto the courtyard cafe.

Nair sat down while the two constables stood behind

him. Nambiar took his seat in the office chair behind the desk.

"You seem to do very well for a business selling tea," Nair said. He nodded at the computer. "That computer of yours costs more than my yearly salary. How long have you been in operation?"

Nambiar looked distracted. He flicked through papers at his desk. "Oh, about a year now. Yes, we're proud of our success. Ours is a premium product, you know."

"Yes. I know."

Nambiar looked up and ventured a smile. "Um, what is this about, Inspector?"

"Sub-Inspector," Nair said. He spoke over his shoulder to Kochu. "Put that tin on the table." Kochu did so, then stepped back. "Can you confirm that is yours?"

The tin was bullet-shaped, the size of a large flowerpot, and finished in azure blue with gold curlicues sprouting sea-green stems and plum-coloured flowers. The central motif was of three camels in a line.

Nambiar picked it up and examined it.

"Yes," he said, "this is a tin of our Russian Caravan blend. It's inspired by the introduction of tea to Russia in the 1600s, when the Khan of the Mongols gave a gift of tea to The Czar. Camel loads of the blend made its way across the steppes, which is what the motif represents." He lifted the lid and inhaled. "Yes. That smoky smell is key. Some tea historians say it came from the campfires that the traders lit, which infused the tea." He replaced the lid and set the tin down on the desk. "That is definitely our product."

Nair nodded. "Very good. And who does your blending?"

Nambiar looked smug. "Why, we do, of course. Our highly trained blenders make it up to our customer's specification. The Sea Queen's man specified it—I forget his name, a fellow from Assam or thereabouts—and we blended it." He leaned forward and placed his elbows on the table. "We have never had any complaints. In fact, quite the opposite. People rave about it."

"Rave. Interesting choice of word." Nair said. "And where do you do this blending? Here?"

Nambiar shook his head. "Why no, Sub-Inspector. We do that at our purpose-built blending facility. On Fort Cochin island. It's then packaged and distributed from there. This is our retail operation. We can't have lorries and sacks coming in and out. It spoils the ambience."

Nair pursed his lips. "All very impressive, Mr. Nambiar. But tell me one thing. If you are such a high-end operation, why does this tin not have the name of your company on it?"

He spun the tin around so the label faced Nambiar. "Look at this. It says 'Forntum & Manson'." Nair's eyes narrowed.

Nambiar gulped. "Well, it's branding. English tea has a much higher value among consumers than Indian brands. So, we adjust our branding to meet their expectations."

"Cheat their expectations, you mean." Nair's voice was scornful. "You call it branding. I call it counterfeit. You're trying to pass your tea off as coming from Fortnum & Mason, isn't it? In London Piccadilly. I checked. That company is 300 years old. 'By Appointment to His Royal Highness, King Charles' it said."

The alarm on Nambiar's face was unmistakable. "No, no, no, no, no!" he cried. "You've got it all wrong-"

"Save it," Nair said. He got to his feet. "You can tell the judge. Get up, you idiot! We're going to your blending place. Now!"

Nambiar shot out of his chair, hands flapping. "Of course. Of course. Whatever you wish, Sub-Inspector. May I just take a moment to inform my manager? So he can cover for me while I'm away?" Nambiar offered a shy smile. "I am very keen to co-operate with you, but I also need to make sure my business is looked after while I'm away. With your permission?"

Nair grunted. "Fine. Outside in the courtyard in five minutes. Don't make us come looking for you."

Nambiar had regained some of his composure by the time he emerged.

"Shall we take my car?" Nambiar said. "It's a Range Rover. Air-conditioned. More comfortable than yours." He nodded at the police jeep, a vehicle that had seen better days.

"Air-conditioned, you say?" Nair pretended to consider the proposal. "No! Get in the jeep, idiot. What do you think this is? A pleasure trip?"

6

Nair rode in the front with the driver, while Kochu kept Nambiar company in the back. They rattled along the roads, making reasonable progress. The jeep headed south down Marine Drive, then turned east at the statue of Mahatma Gandhi. They drove on past the Durbar Hall to Jos Junction, where they joined the flow of traffic heading south down Mahatma Gandhi Road. It wasn't long before they'd left the city centre behind and curved back around the ship yard towards the sea.

Nair cast a glance back as they crossed the Thevara Canal; Nambiar looked as serene as Buddha, as if he were a tourist being taken on a tour. It wasn't the expected demeanour of suspects thrown into the back of a police jeep. That worried Nair but, by the time the jeep had skirted the southern fringe of the Naval Air Base, he'd put it aside. North it was thereafter, reversing the route that Nair had taken that first day when he had received Kochu's call. Jew Town was its usual bustle as was Bazaar Road. As they passed Mattancherry Police Station, Nair couldn't help peering through the gates, as if he might see through the brickwork and detect Inspector Kurien lurking within.

The first sign that something might be amiss came as the jeep crossed the single lane bridge that spanned Calvathy Canal. It was a text message. From Koshy.

'Be warned! Kurien is looking for you!'

NAIR'S UNEASE GREW. He stared at the screen for a moment, then set his phone on silent and tucked it away. Soon, the jeep turned off the main road and plunged into a maze of streets bordered by rows of humble houses. The jeep came to a stop at a warehouse set above a narrow canal. The gates were open, and the vehicle drove through.

Nair stepped out onto compacted earth. The air was thick and humid; what little breeze there was outside did not penetrate. The floor-space was crammed with sacks and cartons. A pair of labourers hauling sacks in a handcart stopped in their tracks at the sight of Nair. Their mouths dropped open as Kochu extracted Nambiar from the jeep. One labourer let go of his end of the cart and the sacks tumbled to earth in a cloud of dust.

Nair glanced at his phone. Only a single bar of mobile signal. He tilted the phone upside down. The bar disappeared. No signal. That was good, he thought. He did not want a signal.

"You stay here," Nair said to the driver. "Pay attention to the radio, in case we need you. Don't move from this spot. Make sure no one gets out. Kochu, let's go. Bring that tin."

Nambiar led the way, the policemen following close by. There was a distinct floral tint to the air, intermixed with the dusty smell of coir and sackcloth. They turned once, then once again before arriving at a row of pre-fabricated cabins, raised above the earth on metal struts. Air-conditioning units studded the cabin walls. Through the tinted window glass, Nair could see movement.

Nambiar turned to them. "We do the blending here, Inspector. It's climate controlled so as not to taint the tea. This way."

No sooner had they entered than a bespectacled youth met them. The young man wore a black T-shirt and slacks. He had a pencil behind his ear. He nodded at Nambiar, his gaze flicking over the policemen.

"Sir," he said. "We did not know you were coming."

"This is Satish," Nambiar said. "He's in charge of our blending. Satish, these officers want to see the Russian Caravan blend. The one you made up for the Sea Queen. Here's the tin."

Satish examined the tin. "Ah, yes. I remember this batch. We should still have some. Follow me, please."

Satish led them out of the Portakabin through a rear door, across the dusty earth, to another much larger structure that spanned the width of the warehouse. He swiped his access card and pulled the door to. A puff of cool air enveloped Nair.

The interior of this cabin was utilitarian, simply rows and rows of shelves bearing metallic tins of the same design that Nair had encountered earlier, though these tins were of different colours. Nair moved along the shelves, reading the labels.

"English Breakfast by Hairrod's of London. Litpon Regency Blend. PG Tops Yerkshire Bland. Very interesting, Mr. Nambiar. A lovely, little collection of counterfeits.."

Nambiar spluttered. "Hardly. There is no counterfeit. None of those names are trademarked. We checked. And the blends are entirely our own. No wrongdoing. At all."

Nair fixed Nambiar with a beady eye. "I'll bet you did, Mr. Nambiar. A clever ruse. Alter the spelling just sufficiently to deceive the unwary eye. But not Sub-Inspector Vasanth Nair. I see you, with your Manson & Hairrod's and your Litpon. And of course, the Yerkshire Bland. Let's see what else you're concealing in this tinpot rogues' gallery." Nair pointed at Satish. "Move on, fellow. To the Caravan."

Two doors later, the four men found themselves at the very end of the storage unit, facing the very last shelf, that holding the very last tin of Forntum & Manson's Russian Caravan blend. Satish picked the tin off the shelf and held it out. Kochu raised the one in his hand. Nair studied the two.

"An exact match," Nair said. "Turn them over."

The batch numbers matched. It was as close as they could come.

Nair nodded at Kochu, who lifted the radio, thumbed the button and spoke into it. The reply was brief and garbled.

"Well?" Nambiar said. "Is that it? You wanted to see the remaining tea? What a song and dance, Sub-Inspector. You could have told me and I could have had these fellows bring it to us." Nambiar took his phone out of his pocket. "Thrilling experience, but I must get back to my business. I'm calling my driver."

Nair turned to face him. "Not yet. We're going to wait. A few more minutes of your precious time. Sorry for the inconvenience."

Nambiar scowled. “Wait? What are we waiting for?”

Nair gave Nambiar a sidelong glance.

“Rex,” Nair said. “We’re waiting for Rex.”

7

Rex took a while to arrive. Which was unfortunate. Because in the intervening time, Nair was forced to deal with what he had been trying to avoid all morning.

The atmosphere in the Portakabin had become sullen, the only saving grace being the air-conditioning. Satish stood, ill at ease, hand in pockets. Nambiar slouched into a corner, his presence established by periodic sighs and mutterings. Constable Kochu, not being one to stand on ceremony, sat on the floor. Nair roamed the narrow floor space, studying his phone.

There was a single wavering bar of reception at the very end of the cabin, near the wall, but that disappeared the closer one got to the door. Nair stuck to the doorway as if glued there.

Nair had been expecting the rap on the door, but the person who knocked was not who Nair had hoped to see. It was their police driver. The man stood on the step, staring up at Nair with trepidation. The driver gave Nair a shaky salute.

"What are you doing here?" Nair said. "I told you to stay in the jeep! And make sure no one leaves."

The driver saluted again, from anxiety more than respect. "Sorry, sir! Only I have Inspector—"

Nair interrupted, aiming to overpower the driver with sheer volume. "Not another word! Back to your vehicle!" He raised an imperious finger into the air. "Go on!"

It was no use. The driver knew who filled his brown envelope every week. And who purchased his loyalty.

The driver shook his head, as if in mourning. "Sorry, sir. Inspector Kurien is on the radio. He wants to talk to you now. He said that if I didn't bring you, he'd fire me. He ordered me to arrest you if you didn't come." The driver made haste to make amends as he saw the scowl grow on Nair's face. "Not that I would ever—"

Nair's stopped the driver with a raised hand. "Enough! Let's go."

The pair had barely returned to the jeep when the police van turned in through the warehouse doors, lights flashing. Nair's sinking heart leapt briefly at the sight. He stopped, the police driver ill at ease at his shoulder.

Rex romped out of the rear of the van with all the enthusiasm of an Indian bridegroom bursting in through the bedroom doors on his wedding night. Rex's handler, though, had all the enthusiasm of the other end of the operation, said bridegroom's bride. The handler's face suggested that, like the bride, he had undertaken much aggravation and inconvenience for a brief, unsatisfactory, and possibly painful interaction.

"I hope this will not be a waste of time, Sub-Inspector," the handler said. "It's taken us ages to get here."

Nair saw an opportunity for evasion. He turned to the driver. "I'll go speak to the Inspector. You take them—"

The driver shook his head. "The Inspector said to bring you. So I must bring you. Sorry, sir. I'll show them the way after you speak to the Inspector."

There was no escape. Nair climbed into the passenger seat of the jeep and, with little grace, lifted the radio to his lips. He took a deep breath.

"Sub-Inspector Nair," he said, as slowly as he could.

The reply was a series of barks that only the trained ear could decipher. Nair was well-versed in the style of Kurien's outbursts.

"Nair! You! Bloody! Fool! What! In! Hell!"

Nair held the radio away from his ear and waved at the driver. "Get on! Now! Get on!" Nair waited for the driver, dog and handler to disappear, and for Kurien's ravings to subside, before he replied.

"Good afternoon, Inspect—"

"Don't you bloody good afternoon me, Nair! I had the IG on the phone this morning. As if the DIG wasn't bad enough. Do you know what he told me? Do you, Nair? Do you?"

"Well," Nair began, "I could—"

The reply was a roar. "No! You do not need to guess. Because I'm going to tell you. In person. At the IG's office. Where you are going to go. Directly. This instant!"

"But—"

Kurien's tone dropped to a lower, more dangerous pitch. "No buts, Nair. You will abandon whatever it is you are doing right now. And drive directly there. That is an order."

"Sir—"

"I ordered you to attend to the station. And what do I find? You're gallivanting all over town, intimidating honest businessmen in pursuit of some half-baked theory. Businessmen with connections. Connections that connect to the Inspector General. Bad move, Nair. Direct contravention of an order. So, stop your investigation, or intimidation, or whatever it is you're doing. Withdraw any disposed police assets. And report to the IG's office. Immediately."

Nair said nothing.

Kurien spoke again. "Feigning ignorance will not work, Nair. Confirm. Now."

Nair exhaled heavily, then keyed the radio. "Order understood."

"Understood what?"

"Understood. Sir."

"Very good." There was genuine pleasure in Kurien's voice. "Excellent. Finally, we see the holier-than-thou Sub-Inspector Nair cut down to size. I told you, Nair, your arrogance will—"

Nair gave the transmitter a kick. There was a tinkle, then silence. It was no consolation.

It was a dejected Nair that weaved his way back to the storage unit. He had given it a fair go, and the thing had not quite come off. With a bit more luck, Nair might have seen his way out of it, but the day had turned against him. He wondered what the Inspector General would have to say. Nothing pleasant, he was sure.

A disciplinary panel seemed inevitable. With luck, Nair thought he might escape with suspension and loss of pay. He would have to figure out some way to pay the rent while suspended. However, if Kurien had his way, dismissal was inevitable. Nair knew he was a thorn in Kurien's side, a thorn that Kurien now held between thumb and forefinger. All that was needed was the minimal application of pressure, before Nair was plucked out and discarded.

Climbing the stairs back to the cabin, Nair briefly considered the prospect of the end of his dream of fighting crime. He could swallow his pride and return to the paternal home to take over the family business, as his parents had wanted. There were advantages to that: the attention of several sisters and a mother for an only son, regular laundry, home cooking. However, he would have to face his father's triumphant "I told you so", and swallow the bitter pill of defeat. Also, Nair hated farming, even if his role would be mostly supervising the workers. Nair wouldn't need to get his hands dirty but, Nair realised, it was the getting his hands dirty he enjoyed. Not with real dirt, but with the grime of crime.

No, he couldn't return home. Perhaps he would look for another job, something to tide him over while he figured out what to do. A degree in botany from Kottayam University had to count for something. Perhaps he could teach? If he could make it work for a while, pay the rent, ride this out, he might yet make something of himself. Maybe the Army? Or the Air Force? If not domestic enemies, then international ones? Terrorists, even.

His mood brightened a little at that. It brightened a bit more when he stepped through the final doorway and beheld the scene in front of him.

Nambiar was on his feet, hands on hips, head shaking. Beyond him, Satish crouched down, holding out an open tin of Forntum & Manson Russian Caravan Blend, the mouth of the container tilted towards the dog. Rex was doing horizontal cartwheels, twirling around on the spot like a furry streak of lightning. Rex glanced up at his handler, gave a tiny yelp, a tiny bark, then resumed his radial perambulation.

Nair's heart leapt. "What—" he began, "what—"

The handler turned back, puzzled amazement on his face. He blinked. "Positive. That's an absolute positive."

8

Salman Qasim, Inspector General of Police, sat back in his chair, and considered the matter before him.

Qasim had done well to get where he was. There weren't many Muslim Inspectors General of Police in India, fewer still who had been awarded Honorary Membership of the prestigious Cochin Golf Club. Qasim had benefited from the fortuitous conjunction of hard work, diligence, and good luck. He had got it right, most times; when he had not, he had learnt not to repeat his mistakes. Qasim had become an excellent judge of character; he had developed that most useful of skills: the ability to see a thing for what it is, in its entirety, without distracting details. Applying that skill to the case in front of him, Qasim had to admit that this game was a bogey.

The matter had seemed a trifle when he had taken the call from the heavyweight political representative of a heavyweight industrialist. "I'll sort that out straight away," Qasim had said to the politician. "It should only take a phone call to the right subordinate to resolve."

When he raised Inspector Kurien on the phone, Qasim had been clear about his concerns.

"I've had a phone conversation I didn't wish to have," Qasim had said. "About one of your men. Name of Nair. He's causing inconvenience. Major inconvenience. Call him off. I want you both here. Now." He paused for five seconds. He found five-second pauses focused the attention of subordinates. And inspired fear. Fear, in turn, inspired action. "We'll discuss who gets to keep their jobs. And pensions. At this stage, it looks like neither of you."

Now, though, that apparent trifle had evolved into something of a sore.

Inspector Kurien had arrived, with Sub-Inspector Nair in tow. Kurien had spoken first, and at length. The Inspector had leant forward in his chair, while Nair stood erect behind, hat under his arm. Kurien had pleaded and implored Qasim to mercy, whereas Nair had seemed serene and unruffled. That caught Qasim's attention.

"Well?" Qasim called out to Nair. "What do you have to say for yourself?"

Quite a lot, as it turned out. Nair's account took several minutes. By the end of Nair's tale, Qasim's eyebrows seemed stuck in position, they had been upraised so long. As Qasim reconsidered the thing in its entirety, he had to admit it was ridiculous. But he also could not deny the evidence, so far as it stood.

Qasim's chair creaked as he leaned forward again and pointed the nib of his fountain pen at Nair.

"What have you found? In this tea tin?"

Nair blinked. "We don't know yet, sir. But the dog handler says it's some kind of narcotic or stimulant. Definitely illegal. The dog is trained to respond accordingly. We have sent it to the Forensics Lab."

Qasim tapped his foot on the floor. "How did it get into the tea?"

"Ah," Nair brightened. "That's the interesting part. When the BrewHaHa blenders were making up the Russian Caravan Blend for the Sea Queen, they miscalculated. They ran out of Nepalese. Or Fujian. I forget which. There was none to be had from their usual suppliers. They were all in a bit of a panic. The Sea Queen order was a large one, a prestigious first, and a big deal for BrewHaHa. So they secured a supply of the missing component from another source."

Qasim's eyes narrowed. "What other source?"

Nair took out his notebook and flipped through it. "A lorry driver. By the name of Chacko."

Inspector Kurien spun round in his chair and looked Nair up and down as if Nair were naked. "A lorry driver?" Kurien was incredulous. "Ridiculous. Why would they go to a driver?"

"Well?" Qasim said. "Answer, man!"

Nair nodded. "I thought that too. Sir. But the explanation was not as weak as you might think." Nair flipped a page in his notebook. "This Driver Chacko handles a lot of BrewHaHa's deliveries. He also does delivery work for other blenders on Fort Cochin, not just tea blenders but spice merchants, coffee blenders, all sorts. This Chacko fellow told them he had a few contacts. He said he'd secure what they needed for a commission. They paid. And he delivered the one pallet they needed."

Qasim nodded. "And?"

Nair shrugged. "Well, that pallet has also gone to Forensics, but the dog almost did himself damage when he got near it."

Kurien had been studying Qasim's face all the while,

waiting for his opportunity. Kurien saw the change in Qasim's demeanour straight away.

"But, sir!" Kurien was aghast. "Surely, you're not considering—"

Qasim raised a hand. "I am considering, Kurien, so silence." The IG rose to his feet and turned to the window. Kurien shot out of his chair—it would have been unseemly for an officer to remain seated when his superior was on his feet.

Qasim half-turned. "This BrewHaHa fellow. Nambiar. What do you have on him?"

"Well—" Nair began, before Kurien interrupted.

"Nothing," Kurien said. "At most, accidental receipt of alleged outlawed stimulants. No knowledge, therefore not at fault."

Nair tried again. "Nambiar's a counterfeiter. He tries to pass off his own blends as sourced from abroad. That's cheating, sir."

"Really?" Qasim stepped around his desk. He picked up the tin of Russian Caravan and examined it. "Forntum & Manson. Bad spelling, at most. That's not a crime."

"But sir—"

"No, Sub-Inspector, you have nothing on him." Qasim saw Nair's face fall and Kurien's light up. He went on. "However, Nambiar doesn't know that. Tell him to give up this driver, and we'll let the matter lie. No prosecution for Nambiar. If he co-operates. That's not a topic for debate. That is an order. Clear? And no heavy stuff. Nambiar remains unbruised."

Nair saluted. "Yes, sir!"

Qasim nodded. "Good. Get out there. Track down this driver Chacko. Find out what he delivered. Find out who from. Arrest them all. You have one week. And if you can't, you will close the case file. And take this with you." Qasim tossed the tin to Nair, who caught it easily.

When Nair had left, and the door had been closed, Qasim turned to Inspector Kurien. "Well?"

Kurien frowned. "Sir, you know best, but—"

"Yes, Kurien, I do." Qasim replied, "I know you're due to retire soon. Years of undistinguished service coming to an unremarkable end. I know that. I also know your arrest rates are some of the lowest in the city. In an area rampant with crime. I also know you're hardly ever at the police station. And I know your Uncle Cherian is not without influence, even if he's no longer a parliamentarian. So, here's what I propose. Interested?"

Kurien flushed. "Always. Sir."

Qasim crossed his arms. "You stay out of Nair's way. This case will fizzle out. He won't find anything. Or he'll end up arresting some small-time courier. Regardless, it will end. Officers like Nair need to be given free rein to destroy themselves. The more you try to restrain them, the more obstinate they become. Give them their heads, and they'll come back, tails between their legs when the hole they've been sniffing down contains a snake, rather than a rabbit. You just keep your head down, collect your tributes and fade into the background. I've got enough on my plate without you and Mattancherry becoming a major preoccupation. Clear? Good. See yourself out."

Qasim turned his back on Kurien. He didn't see the Inspector grimace, salute, or leave. Qasim was already on the phone, making the call to Nambiar's benefactor.

9

Constable Kochu drove Nair home. Kochu expressed his amazement at Vasanth Nair's escape from the jaws of police hierarchy. Repeatedly. He stated it at traffic lights. He declared it at roundabouts. He proclaimed it at T-junctions, and Y-junctions, and all manner of junctions in between.

"I cannot believe it, sir," Kochu said for the last time, as Nair got out of the jeep. "I really can't believe they haven't suspended you."

Nair smoothed his uniform shirt down. He had ignored Kochu all the way, and Nair intended to continue.

"Bright and early tomorrow, Kochu," Nair said. "Eight o'clock. Sharp. We have a lot of work to do."

Kochu wagged his head. "No problem, sir." He put the jeep in gear, gave Nair a half-salute, and rumbled off down the road.

Vasanth Nair watched the jeep jostle its way into traffic before turning his back. He strode down the alleyway that lead to his accommodation. The 'Green View Paying Guest Mens Lodging' comprised three storeys of concrete, painted canary yellow, and erected on top of an existing bungalow. The landlord had spared all expenses to maximise profit.

Nair had found it after asking Koshy for places Nair might rent. Koshy had asked his contacts and come up with Green View. The reviews on Google had not been promising. Two stars out of five. “Very bad place” said one. “Landlord is rude behaviour” said another.

Said rude behaviour landlord turned out to be a wizened, now retired, former member of the state civil service, that apparatus of government whose unspoken purpose was to hobble progress. It was with this selfsame spirit that the landlord considered his prospective tenant as Nair stood on the man’s doorstep.

“Nair.” The landlord had chewed the name over. “Hindu.” He peered at Nair. “Job?”

The answer to that had unsettled the landlord. His brow furrowed at the idea of a policeman living under his roof.

“Rank?” the landlord asked. Nair’s response would be decisive. It was.

“Sub-Inspector” seemed to reassure the man. “Ah. Good.” the landlord said. “I thought you were a constable or some such low-ranking, uncouth type. Terrible fellows, all of them. An officer is another matter altogether.”

The room, when Nair had been permitted to view it, seemed hardly worth the rigours of the interview. A generous minded person might have described it as ‘open plan with kitchenette’. A realist would have called it ‘a cubicle with a hob on a slab of countertop’. The bed was plain, the mattress well-used and the ceiling fan squeaked. However, the view was reasonably pleasant, and it was the very first place Vasanth Nair could properly call his own. Nair’s family home had been pleasant enough, but sharing that space with five sisters, two maidservants and his parents for the past twenty-three years had planted the seed of autonomy deep within Nair's heart.

"Shared bathroom," the landlord had said. "One on each floor. It's down the corridor. Keep it clean. No meals provided. You cook yourself. But no fridge. Also, no noise. No radio, loudspeaker, hi-fi. No drinking. No fighting. And no girls." The landlord had blinked at Nair's last question. "Yoga? Well, I suppose you could use the roof. Just don't fall off."

It soon became clear that Nair was not the only tenant, and that the landlord's injunctions against squalor, excess and lust were just exhortations. In fact, the landlord was hardly ever in residence. The landlord, being an enterprising sort of fellow, owned several properties scattered around Kerala, and spent most of the month travelling around them all, collecting his rent.

Nair's first attempt at rooftop yoga did not go according to plan. That day, as Nair clambered up the rusty ladder to the roof, the sight that had greeted him had been less than inspiring. The other tenants had already established themselves. They were all male, all young, all shirtless, and all drunk. They sat in a rough circle on the bare concrete, around a collection of rum bottles, mismatched glasses and half-empty bottles of Koko Kola.

The men's heads had swivelled towards Nair as the Sub-Inspector stepped out. Nair had been wearing his baggy vest and shorts, a yoga mat strapped to his back. The drinkers had already occupied the fairest ground, that between the water tank and the parapet, leaving Nair only a narrow strip in which to begin his Downward Dogs. The tenants had started yelping at Nair after the third repetition.

By the time Nair had worked his way through Plough Pose, Scorpion Pose and Shoulder Stand, the yelping had turned to barks and catcalls. It was as Nair slid out of Warrior Pose he decided he'd had enough. The hooting rose in volume as Nair turned his back and descended the ladder. A few minutes, the clamour rose again as Nair climbed back up, but it died a stuttering death as Nair's epaulettes cleared the parapet. A Sub-Inspector's khaki uniform shirt does not match well with baggy black yoga shorts (hairy legs rarely bolster the symbols of authority) but Nair made up for that with a particular sadistic enforcement of the law around public drinking. By the time he had chased the drinkers down to the ground floor and along the three lanes to the local police station, on foot, with neighbours coming out to watch the procession, it was clear who would rule the rooftop of 37, PuthuVilla Lane hereafter.

It was a fine evening for contortions. The heat of the day had mellowed into a pleasant warmth that greased the joints. Nair worked his way through the ten Sun Salutations. The inconstant rumble of passing buses, the constancy of horns and the conversation of rooks did not perturb his focus.

After the last, Nair took in the delicate pastel shades of a Cochin sunset, framed by undulating leaf and bough. The landlord had planted many trees in the compound, with strict injunctions that the fruit was off-limits. Nair eyed the jackfruit tree. The fruits were ripe; at any point, one might break off and smash in the head off an unfortunate passer-by. Nair thought he might have to make a rescue mission, in the interests of public safety, but first, he had more yoga to get through.

Nair was a follower of the Iyengar school, a system that, being progressive and methodical, appealed to his personality. He had tried most of the other variants. Bikram Yoga had left him a sweating mess. Vinyasa Yoga, with its relentless flow through different poses, required flexibility that Nair lacked. Kundalini, with its focus on energy shifts and breathing techniques, left him light-headed from hyperventilation. So it was he arrived at Iyengar.

By the time Nair collapsed into Corpse Pose a half-hour later, he was sweating freely, but his mind, ever a jumble of injunctions and priorities, had ceased its usual prattle. Renewed, he lay on his back, feeling the ridges of uneven concrete through the thin yoga mat, and considered the darkening sky. A twinned contrail of some unseen aircraft traced a path across the heavens. Nair wondered briefly what it might be like to soar so high above the earth, going somewhere, anywhere. Would the world seem as large? Or would it, by virtue of being reduced to the span of a plastic window, seem spannable?

Yoga complete, it was time for dinner. Nair collected his mat and made his way down the ladder. It was as he closed the door of his room that he noticed his phone was flashing.

17:15 KOSHY: Missed call
17:29 KOSHY: Missed call
17:42 KOSHY: Missed call
17:58 KOSHY: Missed call
18:07 KOSHY: Missed call

Nair swiped to unlock the phone just as the thing began vibrating in his hands.

CALL: KOSHY
Answer?

"Koshy," Nair began, getting no further.

"Khat!" Koshy was shouting, loud enough to drown out the background growl of evening traffic. "Khat! It's khat!"

"What khat?" Nair replied, instantly irritated. "What's wrong with you? Are you choking? I warned you about snaffling all those fried bananas, Koshy. If you must, at least chew in between—"

"No, you rural idiot!" There was elation in Koshy's voice. "I'm not choking! Khat. The stimulant. The illegal drug. Khat. That's what was in the sack. You did it, you crazy yogic nightmare. You were right!"

Over the next few minutes, once Koshy had calmed down, he gave Nair a run-down of what the forensics lab had reported.

"*Catha edulis*. That's the plant. Grows all over the Horn of Africa, apparently. Active agent is the alkaloid cathionine. Symptoms of consumption include euphoria, excitement, increased confidence, talkativeness, hyperactivity and sometimes mania. Just like amphetamine. It's a banned psychotropic under the Narcotic Drugs and Psychotropic Substances Act."

Nair had the phone on speaker while he changed out of his yoga gear. He towelled himself off as he replied.

"Ha! No wonder the old grandfather took up break-dancing. He must have fancied himself as a street dancer in his youth. The khat liberated him from reality. What was the sack confiscated from the blenders labelled as?"

"Ethiopian green tea," Koshy replied. "It makes sense. The driver must have bought the sack from one of his contacts. A contact who didn't realise that what he was selling on was a narcotic."

Nair slipped on a T-shirt. "But who? Where did the driver get it from? There was no shipper's address on the sack, was there?"

"No. Nothing at all. That's the mystery. To solve it, we need to find the driver." Koshy paused. "Or—"

Nair wrapped a lungi around his waist. "Or? Or what?"

Koshy chuckled. "Or, my fine fellow, you could just close the case right here. Kurien will be satisfied. So will the IG. Crime solved. Unfortunately, the perpetrators could not be located. File closed."

Nair snorted. He grabbed the phone and put it to his ear. "And that's it? We just give up. Because it's convenient? No!"

Koshy's voice, when he replied, was distant. "Listen, Nair, if you're going to shout into the phone, at least turn the speaker off. You've almost deafened me." Koshy sniffed. "I thought that's what you'd say. Well, that's fine by me. I heard you got a free pass from the IG. Might as well run with it." He paused. "Though you'll have to manage on your own until I've got this other thing wrapped up."

Nair put the phone back down on the table. "Fine. That's what we agreed. That's what we'll do. And how did you find out about the IG?"

Koshy took a long breath in. "Well, let's say I have contacts. Contacts I've been cultivating for a long time.

When I heard the IG had summoned you and Kurien in, I made a few calls. To be fair, I thought that was the end of your brief, undistinguished, and ill-judged career, Nair, but you've got luck on your side. Make the best use of it. Before it runs out."

It was a much relieved Sub-Inspector that stepped out some ten minutes later, dressed casually in flip-flops, lungi[1] and short-sleeved shirt. Nair knew he looked odd; most other young men his age tended to skinny jeans and muscle T-shirts, but Nair was far above any such considerations. He bade a 'Good evening' to the pensioner across the road watering his roses, side-stepped a puddle to avoid being splashed by a reckless scooter and tiptoed past the gate that contained (barely) a pair of insane Pomeranians.

Jinson's Thattukada[2] stood on the corner at the end of the lane, just proud of Palarivattom Junction, where National Highway 41 from the east crashed into the North-South flurry of National Highway 66. It was a wonder that the shop still stood, being a single room just big enough for a refrigerator, a countertop, two kerosene stoves and a hot plate. The non-stop rush of lorries rumbling past should have brought the makeshift roof crashing down, but something otherworldly protected the shop. Perhaps it was the proximity of the mosque across the road, or the temple a few paces on, or the church to the west. Nair rather fancied the idea of the Muslim god and Lord Ayyapan[3] and St. John The Baptist working in silent concert against the relentless degradation of traffic. The eating area was a ramshackle collection of plastic tables and chairs that shared the porch space with an elderly woman who sold paan and cigarettes from a glass case.

It was peak time. There was already an untidy gaggle of young male office workers lounging on their parked bikes, waiting for their orders, most lost in their phones, some smoking. None paid the Sub-Inspector any notice, which suited Nair just fine.

He wandered up to the counter, filling the client-shaped gap between stacks of egg cartons on one side and a puttu[4] steamer on the other. Jinson was hard at work on the hotplate, laying out Kerala parottas[5]. His brother-in-law Johnson was ladling curry out of an aluminium pot onto a steel plate covered with a fresh banana leaf.

Jinson's face lit up when he saw Nair.

"Hallo, Inspector," Jinson shouted, raising a steel spatula. "Ordering something?"

Nair had to raise his voice to be heard over the steamer's hiss. "The usual. Thanks."

Jinson nodded. "Puttu and kadala[6] curry. Coming up. Anything else, sir? We have some very nice fish. Fresh. Just landed this morning."

Nair frowned. "Jinson, you know I'm vegetarian."

Jinson flashed him a grin. "Oh, sorry. I forgot."

Johnson spoke up from his station. "Inspector Sir, you know my father was a vegetarian. But he ate fish. He used to say fish is a vegetable."

Nair scowled. "Was your father in a lunatic asylum? How is a fish a vegetable?"

Johnson grinned. He finished ladling the curry before replying. "Well, sir, my father used to say vegetables have more brain power than fish. I mean, if you compare the IQ of a cabbage and a mackerel, sir, there is no doubt which is cleverer. Mackerel is a very stupid fish. So really, it is a vegetable."

Jinson cast his brother-in-law a glance. "Ignore him, Inspector. Madness runs in his family. Except for his sister. Who I married."

Johnson continued, undeterred. "Why not try, Inspector? Look, I'll put a little package of fish gravy in with your puttu. Just the gravy. Free. No charge. If you don't like it, the next meal is free."

Jinson looked alarmed. "No, no, no. What's wrong with you? The Inspector said—"

"No," Nair said, surprising himself. "No. I'll take your offer. Why not? Where's the harm?"

Nair walked back in the dark, the banana leaf-wrapped parcel warm under his arm. He wondered what his mother would make of his transformation. How quickly had the upright vegetarian succumbed to temptation. It was exactly what she had warned about as he left home.

"First, meat. Then, liquor. Then, women. The steps leading down into Hell. Be careful, Vasanth. Be very careful!"

She hadn't, however, said anything about fish.

"Where's the harm?" Nair said to himself.

The curry had been so good that he had finished the lot, licking the banana leaf clean. The gravy was tangy, spicy, and sour. It had settled whatever parts of Nair yoga hadn't touched. As he lay in bed later that night, replete, Sub-Inspector Vasanth Nair considered again whether fish might qualify as a vegetable. If it wasn't, he thought, it bloody well should be.

10

At 10.37am the next day, the police jeep carrying Sub-Inspector Nair, Constable Kochu and police driver Narayan, turned off the northbound National Highway 966A onto the Moolampilly Bridge. The day had started off sultry, but a skirmishing party of thundercloud had invaded on a quickening breeze and, just as quickly, dispersed westwards. The sudden downpour had tempered the heat of the day and rendered the lush vegetation dewy.

Nair sat in the passenger seat, his left foot riding on the running board. Narayan was a vigorous driver but his enthusiasm had cooled after a sudden turn had almost unseated the Sub-Inspector into a ditch. As they rumbled across the bridge, Kochu stuck his head forward from the galley seat in the rear.

"Nothing, sir," Kochu said. "CyberCrime report still no activity on Driver Chacko's phone."

Nair grunted. "Three days since the last. Not a good sign. No doubt that scoundrel has got wind that we're on to him. He's probably fled. Are you sure the address is good?"

Kochu shrugged. “That’s the registered address on his SIM card, sir. Address may be a fake.”

“Unlikely,” Nair replied. “He’ll have needed to provide two forms of ID for the SIM card. Difficult to fake both. Anyway, it’s a nice day for a drive.”

The smoke and noise of the city lay far behind. On either side, the great sweep of the Periyar River made a mockery of the puny bridge that straddled it. The red tile roofs of dwellings far below were barely visible beneath the canopy of coconut palms. Chinese fishing nets dotted the Periyar’s banks, looking for all the world like spider webs beneath the arched limbs of their wooden superstructure. As Nair watched, a man walked along the beam of one, his weight causing the apparatus to dip with gentle grace towards the water until the net was submerged. Nair craned his neck to follow, but the turn in the road was upon them and the view lost as the jeep dipped down behind trees.

An instant later, they were hurtling along a narrow causeway, flanked on either side by fields of rice paddy. Green shoots rose above the waterline. Women, half-bent, waded through the mud, their hands full of seedlings. Nair’s toes curled in recollection at the sight.

Nair’s father had believed that the landowner should understand the earth, which was why he had despatched young Vasanth to the paddy fields under the supervision of the foreman, Vishnu Chetan. Nair had been taught how to drive the buffalos across the water-logged fields, wading behind the plough. Nair had broadcast the seed into the mud. Weeks later, he had waded through it with the women, plucking out and spacing the young seedlings once they had erupted into growth. He had helped to flood the fields, then drain them, then flood them again. Later, he had joined the women to harvest the bounty, sickles in hands. Nair had been spared having to do the threshing.

"You will always have people for that," Nair's father had said. "Besides, it's women's work."

Nair had not pointed out that much of what he had done had been women's work. And that he had hated every single moment. However, the sight of flooded fields verdant with green made his hot feet ache for the cool suck of mud.

His attention returned to the present. Narayan had brought the jeep to a stop in front of a shack with a thatched roof. A hand-painted sign declared this to be "Homely Meals". A woman was hard at work within, stirring steel cauldrons over a wood fire.

"I have to ask the way, sir," Narayan said, getting out. "This area is just a series of lanes. There are no road names." He returned in a minute, the woman craning her head to follow them as they took off.

The lanes were narrow, bounded on either side by rendered brick walls and fences. The houses beyond were all bungalows, most built of stone and concrete, the walls painted corn yellow, pistachio green or mandarin orange. There was no other traffic, except for a solitary cyclist labouring through the mud. Two turns brought them to a white-washed church built in a style that could only be described as Indo-Futuristic. The facade was an incongruous intersection of geometric shapes that defied the laws of physics.

"Right at the church was what she said." Narayan grunted as he jerked the steering wheel round.

They veered onto a rutted track that plummeted down a defile fringed by coconut palms. The engine groaned as the jeep teetered from side to side around gaping potholes. The hot smell of brake pads filled the air. Nair cursed under his breath and held on tight as Narayan clanked down through the gears. The track ended at the water's edge where a pair of shacks flanked a shallow jetty.

"How the hell does a lorry get through this?" Kochu called, hanging on to the roof struts. "Madness!"

"The one on the right," Narayan said. "There. You can see where the lorry was parked."

The house on the right was humble, its walls mossy bare brick under a thatched roof. Between it and the river bank lay a rectangle of lorry-sized bare earth, tire tracks clearly visible.

The policemen dismounted just as the neighbour emerged from his house opposite. The man was bare-chested, wore a purple lungi and held a toddler to his chest. He stared at them, open-mouthed, as Kochu rapped at Driver Chacko's door. Narayan, no slouch, tramped crossed the bare earth and disappeared, heading to the rear of the dwelling. Nair peered in through the gaps between the sagging window shutters, as Kochu hammered on the door again.

"Police!" Kochu shouted. "Open up!"

Nair glanced back at the neighbour. The man quailed, clutching the toddler before him like a shield.

"Well?" Nair said to the man. "Are they here, or not? Speak up, fellow."

The neighbour shook his head. "They're not there, sir. They have left."

Nair scowled. "Put that child down, man. Come over here."

The neighbour grimaced. His wife emerged appeared in the doorway, alarm on her face at the sight of the police. The man almost flung the toddler into her hands before running over the undergrowth towards them. He wiped his hands nervously on his lungi.

"Who are they?" Nair said. "And where have they gone?"

"Annamma. And the two children." the neighbour replied. He came to a stop two arm's lengths away from Nair. "They left. Three days ago."

"What do you mean 'left'?" Kochu had joined Nair. He stepped up to the man and poked him in the shoulder. His tone warned of violence. "Left where?"

The man clutched his hands in front of his chest in supplication. "Please, sir, I don't know. Just, they left in a hurry. Chacko came back in his lorry. It was the middle of the night." The man gulped. "That is not unusual. Chacko often works late. But an hour later, there was clanging and clanking. I looked out and saw them throwing things into the back of the lorry. Furniture. Some pots and pans. Household things. Then she got in with the children. And they left. The children were crying." The man shook his head. "I called out to them, sir, as they left, but they did not stop." He shrugged. "I haven't seen them since."

Nair spat into the earth. "Kochu, take his details. Get the whole story. Details of the lorry. Everything."

There was a creak from behind. The front door of Driver Chacko's house swung open. Narayan emerged, his trouser cuffs muddy. "It's empty, sir. I forced the rear door. There's nothing of value inside. Just a bed frame and an old kerosene stove. Everything else is gone."

Nair followed Narayan in. The house was shabby and old, but the floor had been recently swept, and there were no cobwebs in the eaves. The thatch seemed to be in good condition. Nair flung open the shutters, but the flood of light did nothing to improve their chances.

"What's out back?" Nair asked.

"A yard." Narayan said. "Where they did their laundry. There's a bucket. And a clothesline. And a half bar of laundry soap."

The patch at the back was rough earth but once tended—there was a neat border where the progress of undergrowth had been checked by the application of a hoe. Nair looked inside the bucket, twanged the clothesline, and wandered around the yard in a morose mood. There was sourness in his throat. They had come so close, but now, with the driver and his family gone, the case had stalled again. The future loomed black.

"Maybe the neighbour has another address," Narayan said over his shoulder. He was closing the window shutters. "Or maybe the driver rents this plot. The Land Registry might have details of the landlord's address."

Nair nodded, shrugged. "Maybe. Maybe." He stopped short. His eye fell on something in the far corner, hard by a bank of earth. "Narayan, come here a minute."

The two men made a beeline for what Nair had seen. Narayan squatted down and sifted through the earth with his bare hands. He glanced up at Nair.

"Ash," he said. "Something was burned here. Stinks of kerosene. Looks like paper. Look, here's a piece."

Nair took the fragment. "You're right. Paper. This is some kind of receipt. Handwritten. Blue ballpoint ink. But just a corner. Anything else?"

Narayan got to his feet. His hands were black with soot. He held out another pale blue shred. "Nothing else. Just this." Narayan rubbed his hands together, grimacing. "Ugh. I need to wash my hands. Excuse me, sir."

Nair held the strip of paper up to the light. It had been torn up before it was set alight. There was a single line of printed lettering still visible. Holding it between forefinger and thumb, Nair made his way around the house to the jeep. He retrieved a plastic evidence bag from the store under the seats and slipped the paper in it.

Narayan returned from the jetty, his hands wet, a bar of soap clutched in one. “Borrowed it from the neighbour,” he said. “Better return it. Any luck, sir? Bit of a wasted trip, no?”

“I’m not so sure, Narayan.” There was a slight smile on Nair’s face. “I’m not so sure.”

It didn’t take Kochu long to interrogate the neighbour. The constable emerged, blinking, into the sunlight just as Nair and Narayan were tacking police tape across the door.

“These country houses,” Kochu said, shaking his head. “Primitive. No electricity. Water from the river.”

“Never mind all that,” Nair said. “Did you get anything useful?”

Kochu nodded. “Photo of the driver and his family. Neighbour took one of them altogether at Onam[1], after church.” He held his phone up. “He’s sent it to me. Also, one of the lorry. But no licence plate in that shot. Chacko was very proud of the lorry. Said that he part owned it. Said his boss had given him a loan to buy it. That was two years ago.”

“Any idea who this boss was?” Narayan asked.

Kochu shook his head. “No. Some big-shot in Cochin.”

“Which means,” Nair said, “Chacko is still working for that big-shot.”

Kochu looked puzzled. “How, sir?”

Nair frowned. “Think about it, Kochu. If you’re a businessman, and you put down a payment for a lorry that your driver is going to pay off in instalments, how long do you think it would take for the driver to pay it off?”

"Oh." Kochu scratched his head. "Well, years. Ten? Twenty? Yes, years."

"Exactly. The neighbour said Chacko had got the lorry two years ago. So Chacko must still work for the same guy."

The two constables nodded. Kochu spoke first. "But how do we find this owner? The lorry is gone."

Narayan spoke up. "Run it through the Regional Transport Office register. You have the make, model and colour. They should be able to come up with a list. We then narrow down the list until we find the owner."

"Exactly," Nair said. "Let's go. Kochu, you call it in while we're moving."

They leapt into the jeep. Narayan shifted into reverse and swung the jeep around, pointing it up the track. The neighbour and his entire family had come out to watch the police depart. The toddler waved 'bye bye' at them. Kochu waved back.

"Where to now, sir?" Narayan said, as the vehicle ground forward.

Nair was studying the shred of paper in the plastic envelope. "Back to Cochin. To St. David's Lane. In Kacheripady. Step on it."

II

St. David's Lane lay just off Banerji Road, the main artery that ran east from Marine Drive to become National Highway 66. It was half past lunchtime by the time they approached. Nair stuck his head out and fanned himself with his hat, while the traffic stopped. And started. And stopped.

The entrance to the lane was flanked by St. David's Convent on one side (gates appropriately forbidding to deter unauthorised entrance) and a Punjabi dhaba[1] on the other. Once they turned in to the lane, they were immediately under shade, and the world seemed a cooler, saner place all at once. The lane was just wide enough for the jeep, bounded on either side by the walls of the residences that flanked it. The houses belonged to a bygone age, boasting a distinct lack of steel and glass, set well back from the road in well-maintained gardens. Most, if not all, of the gardens bore magnificent trees, and it was the canopy of these, intermingling high above, that gave St. David's Lane its saintly serenity.

The jeep crawled forward, the growl of its diesel engine

amplified tenfold by the echo off the walls on either side. Police heads scanned left and right.

"What are we looking for?" Kochu asked. "Lorries?"

"Unlikely," Narayan replied, riding the clutch. "This is a residential area. I don't see any lorries. Quite a few cars. Scooters. But no lorries. Anyway, this road is barely wide enough for a jeep. How would a lorry get in and out?"

Nair said nothing, chewing at his lip in frustration, an emotion that transformed into annoyance as the jeep came to a sudden halt and Nair's head nearly hit the windscreen.

"Sorry, sir!" Narayan said. "I was looking right so much I forgot to look ahead!"

The jeep had stopped short of a pair of grand iron gates that marked the end of the lane. Beyond the gates lay a grand manor, two sprawling stories under a black-tiled roof, festooned with balconies, columns and porticos. The grounds were equally palatial, the footprint at least four times that of the other houses in the lane. Nair counted the fruit trees.

"Three mangoes. Four jackfruit. Two, no three papaya. And guava. It's a veritable orchard!"

Kochu read the name set into the gate in iron curlicues. "Amber Villa. Odd name for a house."

"Never mind that," Nair said. "Out! All of you! I mean, both of you! Out and ask around!"

Narayan turned the engine off as Kochu scrambled for the tailgate. Nair had just set one foot to earth when Narayan called out to him.

"Sir!"

Nair fixed him with a glare. "What?"

Narayan quailed. "Just a question. What are we asking about?" He paused before venturing further. "Lorry, is it?"

If Nair were a volcano, he would have rumbled. "I don't

know! You're a policeman, aren't you? Use your instincts! Just ask! If it has to be lorries, then yes, ask about lorries!"

The two constables fled towards the far end of the lane, deciding that it would be safest to put some distance between themselves and the irritable Sub-Inspector. Nair watched them retreat, then turned his attention to his end of the lane.

Peering through the bars protecting Amber Villa, Nair could just about make out the car porch. There were three vehicles parked there, one a silver-grey Mercedes sedan with tinted windows, the second a black Audi SUV and the third a BMW sports coupe. There were air-conditioning units on the balconies. All the windows were closed. The grounds were immaculate and far more extensive than they first appeared.

There was no call button, no letterbox, no nameplate. Very unusual. Each of the other houses they had passed had at least one of the three. There was, however, a single CCTV camera atop the gatepost, trained on the approach. Which meant there must be someone watching it. Or paid to be watching it.

Nair slipped his truncheon off his belt and beat it against the bars. The clanging was fearsome. It took less than ten seconds for a figure to emerge from behind the wall, this a youth wearing a grey uniform (with epaulettes, no less). The youth had bothered to take the time to set his hat on his head. There was a logo on the youth's left breast pocket that Nair couldn't quite make out.

The youth raised an insolent chin at the Sub-Inspector.

"What?" the youth said to him. "What do you want?"

Volcano Nair began smoking. "What do you mean 'what do you want', you idiot? Can't you see who I am?

Police! Come over here! Now! Open the gate! That's an order."

The youth tilted his head at Nair, lifted a walkie-talkie to his lips, muttered something into it, listened, then sauntered over.

"Faster, idiot!" Nair sputtered. "I haven't got all bloody day!"

"What you want?" the guard said. Nair could see he was of Nepalese extraction. He was short and stocky. The logo on his shirt was of some sort of thin chicken. The lettering underneath said 'EAGLE SECURITY.'

"I told you to open the gate!" Nair said. "Get to it!"

The youth shook his head. "No."

"No! What do you mean, no? I'm the police. Open this gate now!"

The guard raised an eyebrow at him. "You got searching warrant? You show. No searching warrant, no gate open."

Nair's eyes narrowed. "I don't have a warrant. I want to ask you some questions. I am the police! Open the gate!"

The guard spoke into the walkie-talkie again. "No warrant, you no coming in. You also no question asking. This private. Private ground. You not touch gate. That private gate. You make noise, my boss telephone police boss." The guard raised a finger at Nair in warning. "My boss big boss, okay? He know big, big police boss. You small, small policeman. You go is good for you, ok?" The guard shooed him away. "You go now, small policeman. Bye bye."

Nair considered angles and trajectories. He thought it just possible that he might fling his truncheon overhand through the bars and hit the guard in the head. However, that begged the question of how Nair would scale the gate to retrieve his truncheon. As Nair contemplated this puzzle, the guard turned his back and ambled off.

Fuming, the Sub-Inspector spun around on his heel, to be met by a pair of eyes regarding him from on high, just above the boundary wall of the property adjoining. The eyes were rather rheumy, the eyelids wrinkled, the forehead above glistening and hairless, which features extended upwards onto the bald pate. The old man seemed to be seven feet tall, judging by the height of his bare shoulders above the wall.

"O-ho," spoke the head in a surprisingly powerful voice. "Postman, eh? Not had much luck, eh? Glad to see it. I, too, have had little luck." A hand appeared and fitted a pair of spectacles onto the beaky nose. The eyes blinked at him. "Oh, I see now. You are actually a policeman. I thought you were a postman. Same khaki uniform, you know. My eyesight is not so good these days."

Nair, not one to let a statement go unchallenged, was lost for words. The head disappeared behind the wall. A few instants later, the gate swung open and the elderly gentleman reappeared, holding a pair of shears. In person, he was barely five feet tall. He wore ragged, knee-length brown shorts and a threadbare banian.

"I was pruning the tree," the old man said. "It requires a ladder. My wife worries about me climbing ladders at my age, but I say to her 'If I'm going to die, Mariamma, I'd rather die falling off a ladder than decaying in a hospital bed.' I hate hospitals." The old man peered at Nair. "Do you, by any chance, play chess?"

Thus it was that, ten minutes later, Sub-Inspector Nair found himself in the living room of Dr. and Mrs. K. K. Eapen, studying the chessboard in front of him and considering how best to respond to Dr. Eapen's opening moves.

Nair thought he had it figured out when Mrs. Eapen arrived with a cup of hot tea and a plate of steaming parippu vadas[2].

"Don't distract the Inspector, woman," Dr. Eapen said, as his wife scurried away. "Chess is a serious business. Your move, Inspector, but please don't feel any pressure. Take all the time you like. We retired people have all the time in the world."

Nair took a sip, bit into a vada, gasped at the heat of green chilli, and reached for a pawn. "Thanks," he said. "What did you mean when you said you too had had little luck, Dr. Eapen? With your neighbour, did you mean?"

Nair's fingers had barely set his chess piece down before Dr. Eapen reached for his knight.

"Your move, Inspector," Dr. Eapen said, placing his piece. "Oh, just that I too have been unsuccessful in making the acquaintance of the gentleman next door. Though I have lived here for forty-three years, and he just for three years and three months, yet I am no closer to putting a face to the house, let alone a name to the face. Or a name to the house. Or even a face to the house."

"Aha," Nair said. Dr. Eapen's knight now threatened two of Nair's pawns. Nair moved one. "Not a neighbourly type, your neighbour?"

"No," replied Dr. Eapen. Another lightning fast move. Nair lost a pawn, and now one of his bishops was at risk. "Your turn, Inspector."

"Sub-Inspector," Nair said. "I have many years before me to reach Inspector." With three pawns deployed, and one already lost, Nair thought he'd try a knight of his own.

"Oh, for a man of your good looks and obvious intelligence, only months, surely?" Dr. Eapen nodded at Nair's move. "Ah. Yes. A strategic move. Playing the long game, eh?" He chuckled. "Now, let me see."

By the time Dr. Eapen had pincered Nair's king, the Sub-Inspector had learnt that the neighbours in the big house kept to themselves, that attempts at introduction had been rebuffed by the gate guard and that no lorries had ever entered or left the premises.

"Quite ridiculous, Inspector," said Dr. Eapen, setting up the board again. "A lorry couldn't even make it down the lane. Why don't you play white this time, Inspector? White may be your colour."

Seven minutes on, after Dr. Eapen had demonstrated the Sicilian Defence, Nair had learned little more of use, except that all the other residents of St. David's Lane had lived there for decades.

"Mostly older people, Inspector," said Dr. Eapen, "either nearing retirement or retired. Dr. Shetty at the very end is the youngest. I think. Dentist. His children have left for University. Dentistry also. We all get on very well." Dr. Eapen frowned at the board. He slid his castle along the length of the chess board. "Ah, yes. I think that is check-mate, Inspector."

"Ah, well," Nair said, making to rise, "bad luck, eh? Thanks for the games, Dr. Eapen—"

"What's the hurry? What's the hurry?" returned the good doctor, waving Nair down. "Your men are still doing the rest of the houses, correct? Sit down, sit down. Let them do the work, Sub-Inspector. Good practice for when you make Inspector General of Police—you'll have to delegate. Time for another game or two, I think?" He turned and yelled over his shoulder. "Mariamma! Any more snacks? These vadas are cold."

By the time Kochu and Narayan entered Dr. Eapen's

residence, Sub-Inspector Nair had polished off another cup of tea, half a bowl of ethakkappam and had himself been polished off thrice by Dr. Eapen in a variety of new and interesting ways. Constable Kochu eyed the remaining snacks on the tabletop with interest.

"Come in! Come in!" cried Dr. Eapen. "Perhaps your men would like some snacks, Inspector? Do any of you play chess? Mariamma!"

Nair leapt to his feet, slightly unbalanced by the additional load above his belt. "No, no, doctor! Very pleasant and useful meeting you, lovely snacks, nice tea, but duty calls!" Nair turned and waved the two constables out ahead of him.

"Do come back! Any time, Inspector!"

Nair insisted Narayan back the jeep all the way down the lane and reverse out into the road before speaking.

"Well?" Nair said, loosening his belt, "any luck?"

Precious little. No lorries, nothing suspicious, except the occupants of Amber Villa who kept to themselves.

"Probably some very strict Muslims," Kochu ventured from the back. "That is what Dr. Shetty said. Or Jews. That Orthodox type, you know. Or maybe Jains."

"Wonderful," Nair said. "Muslims. Or Jews. Or Jains. That's all you've got? What about Zoroastrians? Or Naxalites[3]? Perhaps they're Naxalites."

Kochu was about to answer, then noticed the look on the Sub-Inspector's face. Kochu chose, wisely, to retreat into his bench seat.

"Drive!" Nair said, with an imperious finger.

Narayan raised an eyebrow and shifted the jeep into first gear. "Which way, sir?"

The finger pointed west. "Fort Kochi. Jew Town. Step on it."

12

They had to stop for lunch. The rumbling of Kochu's stomach almost drowned out the diesel engine, not to mention his exaggerated brow mopping and complaints of feeling faint. Narayan pulled up at a humble wooden hut with a thatched roof, around which were parked a cluster of auto-rickshaws.

"You two go ahead," Nair said, rubbing his belly. "I'll give lunch a miss." As the two constables ducked under the threshold, Nair stepped out and stretched his legs. He thumbed Koshy's number. It took Koshy a while to answer; when he did, there was a sizzling sound in the background.

"Koshy! What the hell is going on? You sound like you're on fire."

Koshy's voice rumbled through the speaker. He was not amused. "Haha, Nair. Always poking fun. What do you want?"

Nair gave Koshy a thumbnail sketch of the morning's discoveries. "Driver's disappeared. Along with his family. And the lorry. They cleared the hovel out. The only clue we found sent us to a residential neighbourhood in Kacheripady. Nothing. Except for a huge house behind some enormous gates. No one knows who lives there. Odd, no?"

Koshy grunted. "Lots of rich people in that part of town, Nair. They don't have enormous gates for nothing. What's your plan?"

Nair scratched his head. "Not sure. Wait for the list of lorries matching the description? In the meantime, we're headed to Jew Town."

"Oh?" Koshy sounded wary. "Really? Is that wise? I mean, Jew Town is like an anthill. Comings, goings. A man can barely move for the crush. What do you hope to find there, anyway? It's pointless. And hot. Very hot. Maybe you should head back to the station instead to—"

"Nothing doing! That driver worked out of Jew Town. He must have sourced the contraband from somewhere there. It's the perfect location. Warehouses. Godowns. Legitimate import-export businesses. Jetties nearby. Lots of contraband makes its way onto Fort Cochin under cover of darkness. It's a full-time job for Customs keeping on top of it."

Koshy sounded irritated. "I'm not sure about that. You'll spend all day working up a sweat for nothing. Better just wait for the licence plate details. Take the rest of the day off. An afternoon under the fan in the station house, working your way through a pile of FIRs[1]. Perfect. Cup of tea. A biscuit, maybe even an ethakkappam."

The mention of fried bananas set Nair's stomach into turmoil. "No, thanks. I've had more than my fill. Anyway, why are you so bothered—"

"Oh. Must run. Trailing a criminal. He's on the move. Bye."

Nair stared at the phone. He'd been hung up on. By Koshy. It was intolerable.

The constables emerged ten minutes later, wiping their washed hands on their handkerchiefs. Narayan didn't need to ask for their destination again. Nair was already in his seat, brows thunderous.

They made good time and, in under half an hour, were threading their way north on Fort Cochin Island, the jeep slowing as the road narrowed. Nair ordered Narayan to turn in off Jew Town Road into the grounds of Mattancherry Palace. Narayan found a spot in blessed shade and turned off the engine.

"Where to now, sir?" Kochu asked. "I've had a look on the map. There are at least fifteen spice shops within a kilometre. New Spice House, Original Spice House, Ginger Villa, Jayanti Spices, House of Spice, PK Spices, JP Spices, New Original Spice Villa..."

"Alright, alright," said Nair, waving the constable to silence. "I get the picture. Plot a route. Let's go."

Kochu looked worried. "On foot? But it's very—"

Nair peered back at him. "What?"

"Nothing, sir," Kochu replied, scrambling out. "Nothing at all."

Nair turned to the driver. "You stay here. Listen out. We'll call if we need you for some high-speed chase." Narayan looked relieved.

By the time they'd done the round of eight spice sellers, Vasanth Nair's head was spinning. It wasn't the architecture; the colonial-era shop-houses and narrow lanes had a faded charm of their own. It wasn't the traffic, which was mostly pedestrian, a happy mix of locals and foreigners. It wasn't even the heat, which an assembly of slow-moving clouds had mellowed. It was the inescapable miasma of spices that hung around every street like phantoms.

At first, the sheer array of spices on display was fascinating. Of course, there was cardamom, clove, ginger, cumin and pepper—no vendor worth his salt would be without these staples—but once you added in nutmeg, mace, turmeric, galangal, curry leaf, star anise, fenugreek and saffron, it became all too much. That was before one stopped to consider the myriad configurations possible once said spices were roasted and powdered. Chicken curry masala. Fish curry masala. Sambar powder. Rasam powder. These and a hundred others were displayed on every available surface, in packets, jars and sacks.

No one seemed to have heard of Driver Chacko. Every vendor strenuously denied having any dealings with the man or his lorry. It was after they had emerged from another fruitless enquiry at Very Famous Spice House (the tenth) that their luck changed.

Very Famous Spice House seemed a bigger operation than most. The shopfront was tiny but the rest of the premises to the rear, guarded by steel bars, seemed limitless. Beyond, the warehouse floor was thick with sacks and pallets.

The proprietor of Famous Spice House had descended from his office up the stairs a bare minute after the police officers began interrogating the salesman. The proprietor was in his early thirties and dressed in a long-sleeved checked shirt and khaki trousers. He had the look of a businessman and did not give his name, identifying himself only as "the owner".

"No, we don't sell tea," the proprietor had said. "Only spices. This is Very Famous Spice House, not Very Famous Tea House. Other people sell tea. Try Authentic Tea & Coffee Manor, just down the road there."

"But there's tea there," Kochu had said, pointing to the display. "There. At least four different varieties."

The proprietor didn't even look. "That is for tourists. Our principal business is wholesale spice export. We don't sell tea. Now, you will please leave. Police scare tourists away. This is an honest business. We don't deal with anything criminal."

Nair marched out in a huff, followed by a glowering Kochu. By the time Kochu caught up, Nair had turned the corner into a quiet lane. The Sub-Inspector was mopping his forehead and looking worse for wear.

"Today is not a good day for police work, sir," Kochu said, leaning against the wall. "Too hot. Also, the locals are not very helpful."

"When has it ever been different?" Nair replied, studying his shoes.

"Maybe we should call it a day, sir?" Kochu suggested, half in hope. "We can always come back tomorrow. Or next week? These shops are not going anywhere."

Nair would have replied except for the arrival of a street food vendor dressed in a lungi and banian[2]. The man thundered around the corner at speed, pushing a bright blue cart ahead of him. The man glanced at the policemen and leaned back, bringing his cart to a skidding halt.

The cart had a hand-painted sign that said

'★ Kuttappan's Famous Fried Snacks ★
★ Ethakkappam ★
★ Traditional Kerala Fried Banana Specialty ★
★ Served Hot Hot ★'.

On the cart lay a bunch of bananas, a pair of knives, three mixing bowls, one full of batter, and a wok full of bubbling oil, set on a lit burner. Kuttappan himself was rather chubby, with a few folds of fat around his middle and a lot of hair on his chest. He had a towel wrapped around his head, presumably as protection from the sun. His beard was a tatty mess. He approached the policemen with a determined air.

"Absolutely not!" Nair said, standing upright. "We're not having any fried snacks. And do you think it's a good idea, you buffoon, to be wheeling that thing about at such bloody speed with a vat of hot oil on it? And a lit flame underneath? You'll set the whole bloody place on fire."

Kuttappan stopped in front of Nair, hands on hips, legs akimbo. He was much too close for comfort.

Nair's nostrils flared. "Idiot. Keep your bloody distance! You're in for a slap if you don't step back!"

Kuttappan grinned. Slowly, he reached up and tugged at his beard. It came away in his hands. His eyes twinkled at the Sub-Inspector.

"Hello, Nair, you yogic hero! How's that for covert surveillance, huh?"

Nair's jaw dropped. "Koshy! What? How?"

Koshy glanced around. "Shush! Quiet! If anyone comes round the corner, pretend you're shaking me down for some free ethakkappams. Now listen. I don't have a lot of time."

Nair and Kochu huddled around as Koshy continued.

"That place. Very Famous Spice House. It's under observation. That's what I'm doing. Under cover." He gave them a wink. "I'm working for Customs & Excise, unofficially, of course. There're all sorts of stuff going in and out of that place. We just need a bit more evidence before we close the whole business down. But the owner's a canny sort. Runs a tight ship. It's been very difficult to find a way in."

Nair blinked. "Do you think he might have something to do with the khat? The contaminated tea?"

Koshy nodded slowly. "Now that you mention it, it's entirely possible. I should have thought of that myself. There's a warehouse around the back, accessed by a lane to the rear. Could easily accommodate a lorry." He hunkered closer. "Listen, Nair, we should join forces. There's a rare opportunity here. You and me finally working together? We could close this case up in double time. What do you say?"

Nair looked at Koshy with suspicion. "What do you have in mind?"

"No time to explain now," Koshy said. "I'll come to yours. Tonight. After sunset. We'll talk then."

He stood back, slapped the beard back on his face and raised his voice. "Ok, ok, sirs. If you don't want to try Kuttappan's Famous ethakkappams, sirs, it is your loss only!" He walked back to his cart in a huff, wheeled it around at some peril then cantered around the corner, giving Nair a wide wink in passing.

"Pity," Kochu said sorrowfully. "I would quite like to have tried one of his ethakkappams."

Nair glared at him. "Well, be my guest. Go on. And while you're at it, tell him his beard is on the wrong way round. He looks like he's got mange."

Nair was just about to reach into his pocket for his phone when it began buzzing. It was Narayan.

"Sir, just got a call from Traffic. They've found the lorry."

"What? Where?"

"Puthuvype, sir, the island just two kilometres north of us, across the Vembanad Strait. The lorry was driven into a mangrove swamp there and set on fire. Some tourists going to the viewpoint nearby saw it and called it in. Local police are there now, along with the fire service."

"How quickly—"

"Quickly, sir. If we take the Vypin ferry from the Fort Cochin terminal, we can be there in fifteen minutes. I've already called the ferry terminal. They're holding a boat for us now."

Nair broke into a trot. "Good work, Narayan. Come pick us up from the lane behind the synagogue. I've got to liberate Kochu from some bananas."

Boarding the ferry was straightforward, once the jeep had muscled its way through the queue of disgruntled traffic. Ten minutes later, they'd crossed the strait. The ferry's gangway had barely touched earth before Narayan gunned the jeep forward. They tore through the town, sirens wailing. The jeep took a hard left onto a narrow bridge. There was a flash of dark water beneath and then they plunged down into the swamp.

The road was the only sign that mankind had ever set foot there. On either side rose mangroves, their twining roots clawing down into the brackish water, leaf and bough so intermingled that it was impossible to tell one tree from the other. Waterfowl took wing ahead around them, an honour guard of feather and claw that marked the vehicle's progress. Despite their speed, there was no relief from the heat, the air whooshing past thick with the torpor of rot and mud.

In the far distance lay the gigantic twinned tanks of the LNG terminal, pale against the azure sea. The road had been laid to service the terminal, but that was not their destination. Instead, the jeep slowed at a fork and swung left, heading south towards the shoreline, rising as they ascended a slope towards the viewpoint ahead.

They came to a stop amidst a cluster of police vehicles and fire engines, strobes flashing yellow and blue. The fire crew were rolling their hoses back in, leaving trails on the muddy earth. Nair leapt off the jeep before it came to a stop, breaking into a run towards the smouldering wreck half-embedded in the vegetation.

A police constable approached at a trot, a tall young man with intelligent eyes and a slight limp. A gold crucifix dangled on a chain at the constable's neck.

"Andrew, sir," the constable said. His eyes ran over Nair's epaulettes. He sketched a salute. "Based at Narakkal Police Station just up the road. We heard you were looking for a truck." He pointed down the slope towards the swamp. "It's there. Looks like it was put in neutral and rolled down the slope. A good hundred metres downhill is what it is. It would have disappeared into the swamp, but the vegetation is very thick. It got stuck. So they set it on fire, I think." Andrew paused. "Someone has doused it with petrol."

They descended the slope with as much speed as was possible. Constable Andrew led, followed by Nair, with Kochu bringing up the rear. It was treacherous. Feet slipped in the mud and tripped over mangrove roots. They slid to a stop by a clump, Nair hanging onto a tree branch while Kochu fished his phone out.

The lorry was embedded in the mud, its bonnet fully submerged.

"Is that it?" Nair asked. "Chacko's lorry?"

Kochu held his phone up, his glance flitting between the screen and the vehicle. "Same model, sir. Same colour. No number plate, though."

Constable Andrew shook his head. "Both number plates have been removed. They must have taken it with them. Clearly trying to hide something.

Nair frowned. "Anything inside?"

Andrew looked taken aback. "We, um, haven't checked

yet, sir. We thought we would wait for you."

Naturally, it was Kochu that was dispatched into the cab. He emerged, trouser legs slick with mud. Kochu shook his head. "Nothing, Sub-Inspector," Kochu called out. "They have cleared it out. Not a shred of anything."

Nair had clambered onto the truck's flatbed. The tilt of the chassis meant Nair had to hold on fast to the struts. Nair climbed back out, approximating an Alpinist's ascent of the north face of the Eiger, sans crampons.

"Here!" Nair called. He threw something through the air. Kochu caught it neatly just as the Sub-Inspector landed in the slush with a plop.

"What is it, sir?" Kochu asked, wiping the mud off the object as Nair trudged back up the slope to them. "I can't make out."

"It's a toy, idiot. A child's doll. Check your photos again. The ones you took off Chacko's neighbour. There. That one. What's that?"

Kochu peered at the screen. "What? I don't see- oh, in the child's hand! Yes! It is!"

It was.

Constable Andrew looked aghast. "Toy? Do you think that there might be children—"

Nair shook his head. "I don't think these rogues would sink that low, but we should do a sweep of the area. Get a few more officers from your station. We'll help. Scour the roads, at least as far back as the bridge. Also, the beach down there. Let's get to it. Also, ring for a tow truck. Let's haul that lorry out of there. Quickly. We only have a few more hours of daylight left."

Andrew nodded. "Right, sir." He reached for his radio. "What are we looking for, Sub-Inspector?"

"Bodies," Nair said. "A man. Or a woman. Only, I hope."

13

It was a much relieved but much dispirited Vasanth Nair that stepped out of the police jeep into Puthu-Villa Lane two hours after sunset. The relief came from the fruitlessness of their search: they had found no bodies, male, female or infant. The low spirits came from hitting another dead end. They were no closer to finding the driver, and without that crucial piece of the puzzle, there seemed no way forward.

Nair watched the jeep rumble off, lost in his own thoughts, until a voice interrupted his reverie.

"Finally! Where the hell have you been?" Koshy accosted Nair from the seat of his Bullet, the machine parked smack dab in front of the gates to number 9. He leapt off the bike and strode towards Nair. Koshy was in plain clothes: loafers, jeans and an Iron Maiden T-shirt that should have been a size larger. He held his phone up. "I rang you. Twice. I was just about to give up." He paused. "Gosh, you look an absolute sight. What have you been up to? You look like you went for a swim in the bay and ran into an oil tanker."

Koshy followed Nair up the stairs and parked himself on Nair's bed while Nair washed up. Koshy surveyed Nair's room.

"This is some hovel, Nair," Koshy said. "Awful. I'm sorry I suggested it. That gas hob there is a travesty. I should confiscate it in the interests of public safety. And that fan?" He pointed at the ceiling. "I would move the bed, at least. Not safe to sleep under it." He grinned. "Listen, anywhere round here good for a meal? I'm famished."

It was only after they'd settled themselves down at a table at Jinson's Thattukada that Nair updated Koshy on the day's developments.

Koshy lit up a cigarette, inhaled, then exhaled. "Not good. No sign of the driver but the lorry burnt out? Think the driver did it? Or someone else?"

Nair waved the cigarette smoke away. "Someone else. Chacko had a part share of that lorry. It was his livelihood, a means of providing for his family. I can't see him setting it on fire. Which means—"

Koshy nodded. "That whoever did it wanted Chacko out of the picture. Any sign of the family?"

"No. I just hope he stashed them somewhere safe before the criminals got to him. Maybe he abandoned the lorry and is in hiding himself."

"Possible, I suppose." Koshy did not sound hopeful. "Any leads on that lorry? Did you check the plates?"

"No plates." Nair said. "They were removed. But the local police extracted the Vehicle Identification Number from the chassis. Kochu put a request in. At least, I told him to. You can never tell with that fellow. Too interested in filling his belly. I'm going to chase it up personally. Tomorrow."

Koshy looked thoughtful. He fished his phone out. "Tell

you what, Nair. I owe you one. Give me the VIN. Maybe I can pay you back."

"Actually, Koshy, you owe me four, remember? Taking Kochu's call when you were supposed to be on duty? One. Sorting out the problem at the Sea Queen while you were frying bananas. Two. Telling you—"

"Fine, fine. One. Four. Who cares? We're colleagues here. Give me the number and I'll make a call."

It barely took a minute. Koshy dialled a number, exchanged a few pleasantries, read out the number out, then rang off.

"Done." Koshy said. "My contact will call us back."

"Thanks. Anyway, that's my story. What about yours? Famous Spice House. The smugglers. What's the story there?"

"Ah, now that's a proper crime syndicate, Nair. Listen."

Customs had been tracking several undeclared consignments coming into Mattancherry by boat under cover of darkness, many of which seemed to make their way to the lock-up behind Very Famous Spice House.

"It comes in by dhow, across the Straits of Hormuz, from Dubai, we think. Dubai's long been a staging point for all kinds of stuff coming across the Indian ocean. Including drugs. The dhows lay up just outside Indian territorial waters. They ferry the contraband to land in smaller craft. Customs intercepted one, which is where they got their intelligence. They set up further intercepts, but then the Coast Guard ships seconded to assist got 'redeployed' suddenly. What a surprise."

Nair frowned. "Are you saying—"

Koshy nodded. "Political interference. Clearly, the Customs operation was impacting on someone's bottom line. And that someone spoke to someone in power with an interest in said bottom line. So the Coast Guard ships were pulled. And Customs had to change tack. Right now, they're working with the Navy guys to gather intelligence, but who knows how long that will last?" Koshy looked around, then leaned in. "However, we've struck upon a bit of good luck. And we might be able to close this smuggling operation down for good. All we need is some sort of hard evidence that there is actually contraband on the premises and Customs can move in with a warrant. Which is where you come in. Well, you and me. If you're game."

Nair was about to answer when Jinson arrived, hands full with plates.

"Alright, Inspector sirs," Jinson said, "here are your orders. Kerala parottas, freshly made, of course. Egg roast for you, sir, and for Inspector Nair, the usual kadala curry. I will be back with the rest."

Koshy tore a flake off the parotta and stuffed it in his mouth. His eyebrows rose.

"Hey. Nair. This is very good. And I speak as someone who frequents a lot of thattukaddas."

"Clearly," Nair replied, "judging from your waistline. If your family is going to be looking for a bride for you soon, then you need to get in shape, Koshy. That bulge is unsightly. Girls these days have high standards."

Koshy made a sour face. "Hmph. And what would you know about girls today, Nair? Tell me, have you even spoken to a girl since you arrived in Cochin?" He studied Nair's face. "Yeah, thought not. Anyway, you don't worry about me. I have a plan. Once this thing is sewn up, I'm hitting the gym. At the moment, all this proximity to fried bananas is counterproductive, but that changes. Soon!"

Jinson returned with another pair of shallow silver plates. He placed one in front of each officer.

"Mackerel curry gravy," he said. "With our compliments. Please enjoy."

Koshy stared at the plate in front of Nair. "Nair," he said slowly, "I thought you were a Brahmin. Strictly vegetarian."

Nair tore a strip off his parotta and dipped it in the gravy. He popped it in his mouth, and chewed slowly, before looking into Koshy's eyes.

"Like you, my dear Koshy, I, too, am spreading my wings. Anyway, fish is practically a vegetable. Enough talk. Let's eat. I'm starving."

It was after Jinson had cleared the plates away, and the tea arrived, that they picked up the thread again.

"You haven't explained your plan," Nair said, taking a sip.

"Ah, yes. That. Listen."

Naval Intelligence had intercepted communications between the owner of Very Famous Spice House, Mr. Peter John, and a syndicate based in one of Dubai's Free Trade Zones.

"One of the board members of the syndicate, an Arab, is apparently coming to Cochin. In a few days' time." Koshy said, with mounting excitement. "There's some kind of meet planned. In person. If we could get in on that meet, we'd have a way in."

Nair was mopping up the last of the fish gravy. "How do you propose we do that?" he said, without looking up. "Just knock on the door, wearing our best Arabic outfit? They wear those long white sheet-like things, right? With a cloth on the head? You'd look great in one of those!"

Koshy made a sour face. "Look. I admit it's not a complete plan. But we've got to start somewhere. And this Arab seems the best bet. Maybe we could infiltrate his circle? Under cover?"

Nair pushed his plate away. "In two or three days? A very long shot. What do you even know about this Arab?"

Koshy scrolled through his phone. "Abdullah Bin Jamal is the name. Forty-two. Businessman. High net worth individual. Two wives. Four houses. Several large cars. He arrives Friday. Afternoon flight from Dubai. First class, of course."

Nair considered the information. "People like that have people running around after them. He'll have someone meeting him."

Koshy nodded. "Yes, here's a message from Peter John, the Spice House owner. It says 'the Amber team will meet you at the airport'. Problem is, we do not know who the Amber team is." Koshy's brow furrowed at the look on Nair's face. "What's wrong?"

Nair had gone quite pale. He sat up in his chair, leaned forward, grabbed Koshy's forearm. "What? What did you say? Amber team? Did you say Amber?"

"Holy Jesus, Nair, what's wrong with you? Yes, I said Amber. Ease up! You're cutting off the blood flow, man!" Koshy massaged his forearm. "If this is what happens when your diet goes off piste, Nair, maybe stick to vegetarian."

"Amber," Nair said slowly, "was the name on the gate of the house at the end of the lane. In Kacheripady. The address fragment we found at driver Chacko's house. On a shred of paper that Chacko had burnt. Amber Villa. That was the name."

It was Koshy's turn to look thunderstruck. "You think? I mean, is it possible? They're linked? The Arab and Very Famous and this driver and that house?"

Nair sat back in his chair. "I don't know why I didn't think of it before. There must be a connection. Look, the spice house is running contraband. The contraband comes from Dubai. Jamal is coming from Dubai. Driver Chacko moves the contraband around. Chacko has some sort of link with Amber Villa. That house in Kacheripady must be the nerve centre of the operation."

Koshy grunted. "Plausible. But it still doesn't give us a way in. Does it?"

Nair shook his head. "Can't see one."

Koshy's phone began buzzing. "Oh, it's my contact in the RTO." Koshy answered the call. "Yes, it's Koshy. What've you got for me, Madhavan? Any luck?" Koshy listened for a moment. His eyes flicked to Nair. "Madhavan, I'm just going to put the phone on speaker. I have another officer with me. I want him to hear what you've found. Hold on." With a neutral face, Koshy placed his phone face up on the table. "Go on, Madhavan."

Madhavan's voice was clear. "I repeat, sir. The lorry is registered to a company called Moopan Logistics. They have several registered commercial vehicles. All seem kosher. No accident history. Taxes all paid. No red notices against any of them."

"And the registered address of the company?" Koshy said. "Repeat that."

"Amber Villa, sir. St. David's Lane. Kacheripady. Postcode is—"

"No need," Koshy said, reaching for the phone. "We know where that is." He ended the call, then stared at Nair. Koshy brought his hands together and applauded softly. "Looks like your instincts were right, Nair. Bloody well done."

Koshy insisted on paying for the meal, adding a hefty tip that made Jinson's eyebrows rise. The two officers walked back to Nair's residence in silence, both lost in their thoughts. Nair used the flashlight on his phone to navigate the lanes, all now dark. It was well past 10pm and most of the residents had either gone to bed or drawn curtains on their nighttime activities.

"So," Koshy said, as they approached number 9, "what's next? Search warrant for Amber Villa?"

Nair shook his head. "Not enough evidence. All we know is that the lorry was registered to the company. And the company is registered at that Kacheripady address. If we confront them, they'll say the driver ran away. Or that someone stole the lorry. And they'll probably have some heavyweight political connections. Last thing we need is for Kurien to get another call from the IG."

Koshy got on the Bullet and pushed it off the stand. He slid the key into the ignition.

"You're right. Maybe we should dig deeper into the company? Cross-check with Organised Crime? Or Fraud Squad? I've got a few contacts there. Good people. I'll get onto it. So? Are you in? Assuming we can put a plan together?"

Nair considered the question. After a moment, he put a hand out. "Yes. Count me in. And you won't owe me anything for that."

Koshy grinned. He shook Nair's hand. "You're alright, Nair. Uptight, rule-bound, but deep down inside, a wonderful chap. Maybe it's all that mackerel that's turned you." He turned the key in the ignition and was about to kick the Bullet into life when Nair's phone rang. He waited for Nair to answer it. The change in Nair's face was obvious. "What is it? Problem?"

Nair ignored him. "I'll be right there," Nair said into the phone. "Do nothing. Just wait for me." Nair slid the phone into his pocket. "Any chance of a ride? I need to get somewhere fast."

Koshy glanced at his watch. “Why not? I was just going to have a drink, anyway. I still owe you three right. Count this as one. Jump on.”

Koshy started the bike. The engine coughed, then sputtered into life, its deep rumble echoing down the lane, sounding like a herd of buffalos on the canter.

“What’s the destination?” Koshy asked.

Nair clambered on. “Hellfire, this thing is loud. Puthuvype beach, just north of the LNG plant. Right next to the lighthouse.”

Koshy slipped the bike into first gear. “Odd place to be at ten in the evening. What’s up?”

Nair’s voice in Koshy’s ear sounded grim. “They’ve found a body. It might be—”

The rest was lost as Koshy slipped the clutch, and the Bullet thundered off.

14

The quickest route was a dogleg, a straight run west until they hit Marine Drive, then north to Goshree Junction, then west again. The drive should have taken twenty minutes. Koshy did it in twelve. The last stretch took them over three bridges in a row; the waters below flashed past so fast that it felt like they were flying. Vypin lighthouse rose ahead of them like a great finger, its beam a ghostly shimmer in the evening mist.

Nair pointed left as they neared. “That way,” he said, but Koshy had already seen the lights of the police vehicles and tilted the Bullet towards the beach. The constable guarding the perimeter took some convincing that the two young men, dressed in denim and lungi respectively, were not just gormless spectators. Koshy had to wave his ID in the man’s face before they could pass.

Constable Andrew ran across the sand towards them. He saluted and fell into step.

“This is Sub-Inspector Koshy,” Nair said. “A colleague. What have you found?”

“A body, sir,” Andrew said, almost jogging to keep up.

"Fishermen found it. Just beyond the breakwater, sir. About two hours ago. They called it in. I thought of you."

"Hah!" Koshy said, puffing hard. "That's about right. Every time there's a dead body, they think of you, Nair. Useful location, though. To dispose of a corpse."

"This is a working beach, sir," Andrew said. "Not a tourist area. Sea fishermen launch their boats from the sands a half kilometre away. There are Chinese fishing nets nearby. Hardly anyone comes here after dark. Yes. It is a good place for such things. Though most of the bodies that wash up here are women." He shrugged. "Suicides," he said, as if that explained everything.

They trudged through the sand towards the seawall that ran the length of the beach. The wall was ten vertical feet of stonework with a walkway set atop. As they neared, they could make out the silhouettes of several men outlined by the frosty glare of portable fluorescent lights. Andrew pushed through the crowd of constables, clearing a path for Nair and Koshy.

The body was male, and entirely naked. Koshy knelt down at its side.

"No visible wounds," Koshy said. "Facial bruising, though. See here? He's been beaten. And look, ligature marks. Around both wrists. But no rope. Cut off before the body was dumped." He looked up at Andrew. "Did you find the body here? It's very far from the water."

"The tide comes up to the seawall," said another policeman. "Today, the high tide was about 6pm. The fisherman found the body after the water receded. It was just as you see it now."

Koshy looked up at Nair. "Is it your man? That driver?"

Nair studied the photograph on his phone. "I think so." He turned the phone towards Koshy. Koshy leaned in, then nodded. "It wasn't a natural death, was it?" Nair pointed. "Definitely not suicide. There's a ligature mark around the corpse's ankle."

Koshy crab walked along the sand. "You're right. Marks around the outside of both ankles, but nothing on the inside of either."

"Which means," Nair said, "someone tied both ankles together. That rules out suicide. If you were going to drown yourself, why would you tie your hands and feet together? And how would you get into the water?"

"Hopping?" suggested a constable. He gulped at the glares he received. "Sorry, sirs. Stupid idea. Sorry."

Nair and Koshy left Andrew at the scene and tramped back over the sand.

"You've got reasonable cause now," Koshy said. "For a warrant, I mean. For Amber Villa. This wasn't a natural death. Someone killed Chacko. Someone tied him up and threw him into the sea. From a boat. His boss seems the prime suspect. The boss who's illicit cargo Chacko had been moving." It took a moment for Koshy to realise that he had lost Nair. He turned back. Nair was standing still, looking east, towards the mainland. "What? What now?"

"You still owe me two, right?"

Koshy sighed. "Let me guess. You want to go somewhere else. Kacheripady. Team Amber." There was no need for Nair to reply.

St. David's Lane was dark and silent. Forewarned by his passenger, Koshy switched the Bullet's engine off just after they turned into the lane and the motorcycle coasted along, the only sound the hiss of tyres on tarmac. A dog barked twice as they passed, then decided it had better things to do. The headlight picked out the bars of the great gate guarding Amber Villa. Koshy braked, bringing the bike to a stop a foot short. Nair peered through the bars of the gate, while Koshy played the headlight across the house beyond.

"See anything?" Koshy asked. "Looks very dark." He glanced at his watch. "Oh, it's almost midnight. Suppose they're asleep."

"Odd," Nair said. "There are no security lights." Nair pressed his head to the metal, peering right. "Where's that insolent security guard? No sign of him either." He stepped back, looking up and down. "I might get over that if you lend a hand."

A sudden glare of light lit Nair up. It came from behind. Dr. Eapen called down to them from up his ladder, flashlight in hand.

"You're too late, Inspector. They've gone. They seemed to be in a great hurry." Dr. Eapen paused. "Care for some tea? I'll wake the wife."

Vasanth Nair convinced the doctor to let his wife sleep as he ushered them into the living room. "It's no problem at all, Inspector. She enjoys having guests. I'm sure she can rustle up some snacks quickly. No? Well, if you insist. Please. Sit. And you too. Ah, another Inspector! I'm honoured, honoured."

It took a moment or two for Dr. Eapen to get going again.

"After you left, Inspector, I made it a special point to keep a keen eye out. I may have mentioned that I have a large jacaranda on the right side of the house, just by the boundary wall between my house and the neighbour's. I have been meaning to prune it but your visit gave me just the excuse. Every day, I go up the ladder and chop off a bit. It just so happens I have a magnificent view of the neighbour's house from up there."

Koshy was staring at Eapen with a bewildered look on

his face. Nair ignored Koshy, his attention entirely on the doctor. "And? Anything?"

Dr. Eapen shook his head. "Very little. Except this evening. A lot of commotion. So I climbed the ladder."

"And?" Nair was on the edge of his seat.

"Luggage, Inspector. Lots of luggage."

"Luggage?"

"Yes. Lots. Being loaded into the back of the cars. They have three cars, you know. Very expensive foreign models. I made notes of the licence plates." The doctor made to rise. "I will fetch them."

Nair waved him back down. "Later. Later. What happened after? Did you see?"

Eapen smiled a canny smile. "Well, I had to descend, of course. Otherwise, they would have suspected. I set my timer for ten minutes. The timer rang. I had just stepped out the door, heading for the tree, when I heard the gates open. I rushed out, just in time to see all three cars speeding down the lane. Speeding, Inspector! At least thirty kilometres per hour. Crazy people. They might have knocked someone down. Old Mrs. Chettiar, for example. She's almost blind, but she insists on walking her dachshund. That dog is almost blind too! Why if she had been-"

Koshy got to his feet. "If you could fetch those licence plate numbers, Uncle, I can make a few calls. This could be important."

Dr. Eapen looked taken aback, then nodded and tottered off upstairs.

Koshy glanced at Nair. "The old boy is crackers, Nair, but you're on to something. Team Amber head out of Dodge soon after we discover Chacko's body. Coincidence? I don't think so. They've either got someone on the inside in the local police. Or someone keeping watch at Vypin. Someone tipped them off."

Nair nodded. "You're right. Except we're too late. Again."

"Never give up hope, Nair. We might still nab them. Ah, thank you, Uncle."

Dr. Eapen had returned. The old man held out a ruled notebook. The cover had the image of a grinning coconut on it, with the words "LIFE IS COCONUT!" printed underneath.

"I've just begun my observations of the neighbour's comings and goings," said the doctor. "I've only filled five pages. I'd like the rest of the notebook back, please, Inspector. Once you've done with it, of course. There's one hundred and ninety-five empty pages left."

Koshy gave Dr. Eapen the kind of smile reserved for the clinically insane, inclined his head, tucked the notebook into a back pocket, then walked out the door. He already had his phone out.

"Well," Dr. Eapen said, smiling at Nair, "quite a lot of excitement, eh, Inspector? Very routine for you, I'm sure, but very novel for old folk like us. Now, how about a nice relaxing game of chess?"

Nair shot to his feet. By the time he'd extricated himself, and gained the lane, Koshy had the Bullet pointing in the right direction. Nair leapt on and waved at Dr. Eapen, who had tottered out to his gate. Koshy kicked the Bullet into life, Dr. Eapen looking strangely bereft as he watched them zoom off.

"Thanks!" Nair shouted into Koshy's ear. "That was a close shave. The old man is dead keen on chess."

"No problem," Koshy said over his shoulder. "Nice man.

Bit weird, but well meaning. Need more of those. Not weird, just well-meaning."

Nair nodded. "Hey, this is not the way back to mine. You should have taken a right."

Koshy grinned. "We're not going back to yours. Yet. I need a drink. And the only place open stops serving at 1am. Hold on to your ears."

15

The place that Koshy pulled into fifteen minutes later was not the luxury hotel Nair had expected. The State Government had imposed restrictions on the sale of alcohol six years earlier, and only five-star establishments serving foreign tourists were licensed to serve liquor. At fabulous prices. They had driven past three posh hotels en route. Koshy ignored them all.

Instead, Koshy turned off the highway onto a dirt path that wound its way between stands of banana trees. Koshy had to squeeze the Bullet past cars and lorries parked carelessly on the verge. The path ended at a rough square of tarmac hacked out of the thicket. Carts and shacks formed three sides of the square, the centre ground occupied by folding aluminium tables and chairs, all illuminated by bare light bulbs strung between trees. A portable generator provided the power.

Koshy found a vacant table on the perimeter, its surface still cluttered with the detritus of the last patrons' meal. Koshy turned and waved. A small boy, no older than ten, ran up, clutching a laminated card to his chest. The boy was barefoot, tousle-haired and bare chested, dressed only in a ragged pair of shorts. The boy's face lit up when he saw who the customer was.

"Koshy Sir," the boy said, saluting.

Koshy patted the child on the head. "What is this, Vishnu? You've grown since I last saw you. Come now, clear this rubbish away. Give the table a wipe, then get us some drinks."

Vishnu gave Koshy a knowing smile. "Special Cola, sir?"

"Exactly," Koshy replied. "Go to it."

Koshy waved Nair to a chair and took one himself as the boy began collecting plates. Vishnu ran off, his cargo clattering dangerously.

"What is this place, Koshy?" Nair asked, looking around. "Odd clientele."

The customers were all men, ranging in age from twenty to seventy. Sartorial style spanned the socio-economic divide, from the khaki uniforms of auto-drivers to the high-end denim of hipsters and Instagrammers. Raucous bursts of laughter drowned out the background hiss of gas stoves under the bubbling woks. The clinking of glasses were the high notes to the palpable bass line of lorries roaring down the highway behind them.

"This, my dear fellow, is Nirvana. At least, that's what I call it. A place where people of all strata of society can gather and mingle." Koshy leaned forward. "And get drunk."

Nair looked shocked. "I can't believe you've brought us to an illegal drinking den, Koshy. We're police officers, for Heaven's sake! And it's half past midnight! It's a working day tomorrow!"

Koshy tapped a cigarette out of its box. “Lighten up, Nair. Or Vasanth? Can I call you that? We’re in Nirvana, so we’ve all attained enlightenment. There are no surnames in paradise.” Koshy lit up and took a drag. “Anyway, what have you got to do that's so urgent? The lorry driver’s dead. The lorry’s been burnt. The boss has escaped. You can’t get into the house. I would chill out.” Koshy leaned forward. “Instead, lend your brain power to my problem. How to get into V Famous Spice House. Ah, this will help your thinking.”

Vishnu arrived with another clatter, this time a steel tray bearing two cola bottles, caps off, and two tumblers. Each tumbler was half full of clear liquid. Vishnu placed everything on the table, then looked at Koshy.

“Shall I pour, sir?”

“Pour, Vishnu.”

Once the pouring was done, Koshy slipped the boy a note. “Keep the change,” he said, to the boy’s delight. Vishnu saluted again, this time clicking his bare heels together, then ran off.

Nair stared at the glasses. “I don’t drink, Koshy. No alcohol. Ever.”

“Ha! And you were vegetarian as well. Until you decided fish was a vegetable. So, apply that same principle here. Consider this cola as just, well, cola. Or fish. Or vegetable. Whatever fits your flexible rules.” Koshy picked up his tumbler and clinked it against the other. “Cheers!”

Nair sat still, arms crossed, frowning.

Koshy set his glass down and leaned forward, both elbows on the table. “OK, Vasanth. What is it with you? What’s with all these rules of yours? Why is there no give in the mattress of your world? What are you scared of? Degradation? Pollution? Corruption?” Koshy spread his arms.

"Look around you. Corruption is everywhere. You can't avoid it. So chill out, and live a little."

"That's the problem," Nair said, nostrils flaring. "It's everywhere. And because it's everywhere, everyone just goes along with it." He slammed a fist down on the table. "How do you expect things to improve if we, the police, the enforcers of the law, are part of it? Someone needs to take a stand. If you won't, well, I will."

Koshy nodded slowly. "I get it. You're one of those. You follow the rules because you hope that by doing just that, suddenly, one day, there will be a click, and the world will fall into alignment with your perpendicular. The forces of law and order will hammer all the ugly curves straight. Has it happened yet? Has it?"

Nair remained silent. Koshy carried on.

"Take Kurien, for example. Lazy and corrupt. Thirty-five undistinguished years. About to retire with a full police pension. Have your efforts corrected that aberration? No. And all those ruffians you arrested and dragged into the police station. Any of them still in jail? No. Take my case. Customs are doing what they're meant to do: catch smugglers. Suddenly, top brass pull the rug out from under Customs' feet because Customs are doing too good a job, and the people in power are not getting their cut. And I have to resort to selling fried bananas in the street. The work we're meant to be doing, we have to do under cover. Away from the prying eyes of our superiors. It's not just me, either. What were you doing that Saturday when this whole tea fiasco kicked off? It was your day off, but you were tailing some criminal. On your own time. Why?"

Nair still said nothing. Koshy leaned over and poked him in the chest. "Why, Vasanth? Why? Tell the Buddha."

"Because," Nair said, after a moment, "because it's the

only way out of this hellhole." He sighed. "You're right. Nothing has changed. And I see nothing will change. At least not while Kurien is here. And when he's gone, they'll replace him with some other incompetent." He looked away. "I was tracking a smuggler. I want to get out of Mattancherry and into Customs. I thought if I could come up with some good intelligence, that might stand me in good stead, give me a way in."

Koshy picked up his glass, then tapped Nair's with his own. "Drink. Drink, Vasanth Nair. You have attained Nirvana."

Nair pursed his lips. His mother's warning sounded in his ears, but he ignored it. He picked up the glass, cracked it against Koshy's, then upended the contents into his mouth.

When Nair had finished coughing, Koshy called for another round of special cola.

"Sip it this time, you fool. Sip it."

Three drinks in, the world seemed much more amenable. Koshy, never one to hold back, became even more loquacious. Nair learned of Koshy's working class background, his government school education, his accidental entry into the police and his determination to subvert the system.

"It'sh your duty, Vashanth," Koshy said, arm raised. "It'sh your duty. When the shyshtem ish broken, when it ish corrupt, it ish your shovereign, shworn duty to shubvert it. Because it ish by shubverting the corruption that one achievesh moksha[1]. Knowledge of the shelf. Freedom to act. Releash from earthly passions. Turn enforshed order into chaosh. And in chaosh comesh liberation!"

Nair applauded, grinning like a loon. "Wonderful. 's really wonderful. Moksha. 's great. For a Chrishtian, you're shpeaking like a proper Hindu. Really wonderful inshite. Shelf knowledge? Ish that like carpentry?"

The two Sub-Inspectors laughed, and laughed, and laughed, until the glasses were empty, and the power was turned off.

16

It wasn't the sun that roused Sub-Inspector Vasanth Nair the next morning, even though it should have done. It was well past 9am. The sky was cloudless. The window was open. The fingers of sunlight filtering through the window bars had traced a gradual path along the floor of Nair's room, up the bed and settled on Nair's face.

If illumination hadn't been enough, the rumbles and snorts coming from the floor on the other side of the bed should have been. Instead, Nair's eyes sprang open as the nightmare that had tormented him ended.

Nair's head was throbbing. His mouth was dry. He sat up in bed and rubbed his head. That was the wrong thing to do. The room pitched and swayed as if Green View Paying Guest Men's Lodge had, overnight, become seaborne. Nair promptly lay back down and the oscillation subsided.

He vaguely recalled tottering towards the Bullet, one arm over Koshy's shoulder. Koshy had been singing a song, a filthy ditty that started with his brother's dog catching rabies and ended with the neighbour getting bitten in a very sensitive place. There was another shard of memory from the night before: street lights flashing past overhead, not in straight lines, but wide, languorous curves as Koshy demonstrated how well he could ride the Bullet. Without hands on the handlebars. While lighting a cigarette. Nair also seemed to remember Koshy preparing to kick Nair's door in when Nair failed to get the key in the padlock for the fourth time. Koshy had missed and ended up on the floor. Then, the dream had begun.

In it, Vasanth Nair was behind the wheel of a black Audi SUV, racing down Marine Drive towards a swamp. Koshy was in the passenger seat, dressed like an Arab. Koshy had his head out the window. He was throwing fried bananas at the lorry they were chasing; the wind snatched the snacks out of his hand. The lorry was on fire. Flames billowed from the cab. The smoke played over their car, smelling of Russian Caravan blend, with a taint of khat.

A voice called out from the back seat. Nair looked in the rear-view mirror and saw Dr. Abraham in the rear playing a game of chess with a corpse. Driver Chacko looked up at Nair and grinned. "Game over," Chacko said. Sea water trickled out of Chacko's nostrils, staining the upholstery.

"Checkmate, my dear Inspector," said Dr. Abraham, as he placed his queen. "Care for another game? It's vegetarian, you know. Quite safe. Quite safe."

Nair shook his head to clear it of the dream's taint. He slid a leg off the bed and encountered an obstruction. He looked left and saw a foot. Rather, it was the sole of a shoe. There was another sole next to it. Nair leaned over and saw Koshy, flat on his back on the floor, legs on the bed, mouth half-open, snoring like a bear and drooling onto his collar. Nair exited on the other side.

Koshy was still asleep by the time Nair had washed his

face, changed into a fresh shirt, walked to Jinson's and returned with a thermos of black coffee. The only difference was that Koshy had turned onto his front, somehow with both feet still on the bed, and now looked like he had landed on the floor after his parachute had failed. The snoring had improved, but the drooling was much worse.

Thirty minutes later, Koshy was fit for conversation, after dry retching into the washbasin, then downing a coffee. His first observation related to the night before.

"Learn this lesson, Nair." Koshy said, lying on Nair's bed. He raised a finger into the air. "Never tip small boys who work in secret drinking dens. They don't expect tips. It goes to their heads. That bloody Vishnu. He must have served us the extra-strong stuff." Koshy wagged the finger at Nair. "For future reference. Never drink the extra-strong stuff."

Nair had found a dark corner on the floor. He sat there in Half-Lotus, wedged between the walls, the steel tumbler of coffee between his ankles. He tried shaking his head a little. It wasn't too bad, so he shook it properly before he replied.

"I really don't understand why anyone drinks that stuff. It's awful."

Koshy propped himself up on one arm and raised the coffee tumbler. "Ah, yes! But what a ride, Nair! What a ride!" Having dispensed that piece of wisdom, Koshy lay back down again and stared at the ceiling fan. "When are you going to tell Kurien your case is a dead end? The sooner you close it down, the sooner we can get working on mine, Nair. That Arab fellow arrives shortly. We don't have a lot of time. Which reminds me. I'd better check in with Kochu, see what's happening at the station. I might need to put in an appearance. Unlike you, the IG hasn't granted me free rein."

Nair thought for a moment. "Why does one require the other?"

Koshy was scrolling through his phone. "What? What do you mean, 'one require the other'?"

"Why," Nair said, "should I tell Kurien my case is a dead end? I have free rein, as you said. I could just let Kurien think I'm still investigating the Really High Tea. While working on your case."

Koshy's head swung towards Nair as if it had come loose. "Brilliant," Koshy whispered. "That's brilliant. And what's most brilliant about it is that the upright Vasanth Nair is proposing to deceive his senior officer. A subversion of the system. In pursuit of true justice." Koshy tried to sit up but decided propping himself on one elbow was enough. "Nair, I'm proud of you. We need to go drinking more often."

Nair raised a finger. "No. Never again. My mother warned me. Meat. Then liquor. One more pitfall and my soul is lost."

"Oh?" Koshy looked intrigued. "And what is that final peril? Maybe I can arrange something. It's girls, isn't it? Come to think of it, I know—"

Nair wagged the finger at him. "Absolutely not. I intend to maintain that last remnant of self-respect. Anyway, I think I have an idea. About how we might crack your case. First, make your call. I need to have a shower."

By the time Nair returned, Koshy was patting his face dry with a towel. "Got to go," he said. "Kurien's due back at the station in the afternoon. Just enough time to get into uniform and pretend like I'm doing some work. Kochu has everything under control, he said." Koshy hung the towel on the bars of the window grille. "What's your idea?"

Nair explained in as few words as possible. "Well, what do you think?" he said. "Will it work?"

Koshy looked sorrowful. He shook his head sorrowfully. "I'm afraid to say," he said, "that it just might." His face split into a grin. Koshy leapt across the room towards Nair, arms spread. "Come to my arms, you yogic genius!"

Nair jumped onto the bed. "No chance! Keep your distance, Koshy. I can smell you from here. And there's dried drool on your collar. You can thank me later. Now, get going!"

Nair watched Koshy run down the stairs to the ground floor, whistling the melody of that filthy song from the night before. Koshy looked up from the back of his bike and gave Nair a last wave.

"I'll make some calls!" Koshy shouted. "Keep your phone on! Things might move fast!"

Nair waved back. "Just make sure you don't move fast on that beast! We can't have Customs' newest recruit's career ended by his falling off his bike!"

Koshy was still laughing as the bike took the turn at the end of the lane.

17

The plan evolved quickly. Later that afternoon, Sub-Inspector Nair, dressed in plain clothes, sat in the bus shelter across the road from the entrance to St. David's Lane. Koshy had rung an hour earlier.

"It's on. My Customs boys are on the case. I'll send you the number. Get over there and keep an eye out. Ring when you see movement, and my boys will do the rest. You're sure the cars are back?"

"Positive," Nair had said. "I rang the good doctor. He was up the ladder on pruning surveillance duty. All three vehicles returned early this morning, just before 8am. Only the drivers. No passengers. And no luggage offloaded. Did you check the flights?"

"I got someone to do it," Koshy had said. "As you thought. A family of four, with the surname Moopan. Took the early morning flight from Trivandrum to Dubai. Must have driven to the airport overnight from Cochin. I'm waiting for Immigration to send me the passport copies, but chances are it's Chacko's boss. First-class tickets. Booked just yesterday. Paid for with a corporate credit card.

Eye-watering amount, Nair. I've got Trivandrum police checking the airport CCTV for confirmation. That will take some time, but I'd say the bird has flown the coop." Koshy must have heard Nair's sigh. "Never fear. The bird will return once he thinks the coast is clear. We'll be waiting. With a big, fat net."

"What if this Moopan alerts the Arab? The Arab's in Dubai. Moopan's headed there. The whole plan will fall through if that happens."

"Hmm. That's a good point. However, there's no direct link between Moopan and the Arab. Moopan works for Spice House. Both have a connection to V. Famous Spice House, but not to each other. Moopan also doesn't know for sure that we're on to him, does he? Yes, his informants have told him we've found Chacko's body, but we have nothing concrete linking Chacko's murder to Moopan's business. My guess is, Moopan will lie low in the Gulf for a few weeks. And return when it's clear we've got nothing on him. Anyway, we can't control what Moopan does. We go ahead with our plan. And hope the cards turn our way this time."

This was true. So Vasanth Nair planted himself in the shade of the bus shelter and waited. The Cochin City Corporation was upgrading bus shelters to a new stainless steel model. The press release had said the new bus stop "will have top quality seats, play FM music from sunrise to sunset, incorporate mobile phone charging points, 24/7 Wi-Fi access and hand-designed floor tiles."

That refurbishment had yet to reach Kacheripady. The bus stand Nair sat in had been built in a style that was more brutal than Brutalist, a slapdash assembly of concrete slabs cemented together in a manner that suggested the builders had had other things on their mind that day. The concrete had fissures in it and the roof wasn't quite level. Nair wasn't sure whether the tattered election posters, accreted one on top of the other like growth rings on a tree, improved on the general appearance.

The only other occupant was a nun, a well-fed woman of sixty, dressed in a pure white habit with a matching wimple. The nun had walked across the road from the convent and taken a seat as far away from Nair as possible. She'd fished a copy of 'Bollywood Bonanza' out of her shopping bag and started reading it with interest. The cover depicted a young Bollywood starlet in a skimpy outfit, bellybutton plainly on view, with the title "I'M DONE WITH MARRIED MEN: MANJUSHA EXPLODES!" Nair watched out of the corner of his eye as the nun rotated the magazine to fully appreciate the centrefold. Nair supposed it was important for those who had devoted their lives to God to remain in touch with real life, so far as Manjusha represented that facet of existence.

A spattering sound from behind caught his attention. Nair swung around then leapt to his feet. Barely two feet away, behind the shelter, facing in, a man in a polka-dot shirt and tight green trousers was urinating against the concrete, beedi in his mouth. The man looked up at Nair. His brow furrowed.

"What?" the man said. "What are you looking at? Never seen a man piss?"

Nair raised a finger. "Hey! That's illegal. Public urination. Stop that!"

The man glared at Nair. "Who are you? Police? Is this your father's bus stop?" After a vigorous shake, the man tucked himself back in. "Or are you one of those?" The man leered at him. "You know, the kind who waits at bus stops to check out the talent." The man made a move to expose himself. "You want to see the talent?"

Nair took a step back.

"Hahaha!" The man laughed. "Oh! That frightened you, eh? Good. Because if I had shown you what I have, you would have shrivelled up and died from envy. Get lost! Idiot!"

With that, the man spat his beedi out and walked off, giving Nair a backward glance. He called out to the nun as he passed.

"Hey! Sister! Watch out for that fellow there! Pervert. Keep your distance!"

Nair would have chased after the man, except that, at that precise moment, a black SUV came hurtling out of St. David's Lane. It turned right and sped off.

Nair fished out his phone. The number was on speed dial.

"Yes?" An unfamiliar male voice answered.

"En route," Nair said. He cupped his palm over the phone and turned away from the nun. "Heading east on Banerji Road. Black Audi SUV. I—"

"We're on it," the voice replied, before ending the call.

Nair ran across the road. His moped was parked outside the convent. He kicked the thing off its stand, leapt on and pedalled hard before starting the engine. The moped's speedometer was an exercise in optimism; it displayed a maximum speed of 40 kilometres per hour but that was only possible if rolling down hill, throttle wide open, with a monsoon as tailwind. As it stood, Nair rattled along at half that, almost losing sight of the black SUV.

Nair caught up with the Audi as it slowed to join the stream of traffic coming off the MG Road flyover. Nair filtered between cars until he was within five feet. The

SUV's windows were tinted black; he couldn't see in. Nair looked around, but there was no sign of a police vehicle anywhere. He fished his phone out and was about to call when the crush of traffic broke and the SUV darted forward.

Cursing, Nair pocketed the phone and cranked the throttle wide open.

Nair might have kept up with the Audi had he not been forced off the road. An air horn blared at him from behind. He glanced back. It was a white Mahindra Scorpio, an indigenous SUV, its bumper a bare inch from his rear wheel. He heard the engine note rise. Nair jigged left just as the Scorpio sped up. Nair would have given it a finger, except he needed both hands to avoid falling over as the moped mounted the pavement.

Once he had regained his balance, Nair set off again. A hundred yards further on, he found the Scorpio. It had stopped, angled across the road, its body boxing in the now stationary Audi. The Scorpio's doors were open. Five Customs officers in sparkling white uniforms had the Audi surrounded. One yanked the driver's door open and hauled the driver out by the scruff of his neck. Nair slowed, just enough to catch the eye of the senior office, a tough-looking fellow with gold braids on his chest and wearing silvered Aviator sunglasses. Nair opened his mouth. The officer spoke first.

"Move along." The tone brooked no discussion. He waved Nair on. "Nothing to see here. Official Customs business. Keep moving." He gave Nair the slightest of nods.

Nair found a gap in the median and made a U-turn, stopping on the opposite side of the road. He dialled the number and saw the officer across the road take his phone out.

"We've got him," the officer said. "Good work." He

looked directly at Nair as he spoke. "We'll take it from here. Koshy is en route. He will be in touch with the rest of the plan."

"Thank you," Nair said. "Tell him I'm going to be slightly busy for thirty minutes."

"Oh?" The officer sounded surprised. "I thought you had no other commitments."

"Just one," Nair replied. "A vulgar fellow in a polka dot shirt."

By the time Koshy found Nair, the Sub-Inspector had almost completed his dispensation of street justice. The ruffian in the polka dot shirt had been loitering on a corner, sipping tea from a vendor and smoking another beedi, his back to the road. It had been easy for Nair to knock him to the ground with a perfectly timed kick to the back of the knees as the moped zoomed past. By the time the ruffian had picked himself up, Nair had parked the bike and leapt off.

"Police!" Nair had said, flashing his ID. "Get on your knees."

A small crowd gathered to watch as Sub-Inspector Nair made the quivering ruffian recite, over and over, how he would refrain from urinating in public places and that he was a very, very bad boy indeed. This done while bowing, repeatedly, hands upraised in prayer before Sub-Inspector Nair.

The black Audi pulled up level with the spectacle. The passenger door sprang open.

"Get in!" Koshy shouted from the driver's seat. "Quickly! The air-conditioning is on! You're letting the heat in."

"Don't let me see you ever again!" Nair said, as farewell to the kneeling villain, before turning his back and climbing into the vehicle. He had barely closed the door before the SUV leapt forward.

"Bloody hell, Nair! Can't you ever ignore these passing idiots? What did he do? Whistle at a girl? Spit paan? Let me guess—he walked rudely."

"Public urination," Nair replied. "Intolerable. Behind a bus stop. And there was a nun sitting there! I should have charged him for indecency."

Koshy blew his cheeks out. "Keep your eye on the prize, Nair. If you stop to prosecute every misdemeanour we come across, you might blow this game wide open. Promise me, will you, that you will not play at police officer until we wrap this thing up? Promise."

Nair pouted. "Fine. Fine. I promise." He looked at Koshy. "What did you do with the Audi driver?"

Koshy smiled. "Ah. Arrested. Under suspicion of transporting contraband. They'll hold him. For as long as necessary."

"And how long is that?"

Koshy grinned. "As long as it takes. Takes us, that is, to figure out how to crack Famous Spice House. Your plan is good." Koshy patted the steering wheel. "This little number here is Part One of Plan A. It's the first time, Nair, that one of your schemes has us enjoying a bit of luxury. Look at this car. Not just air-conditioning but individual climate control zones. Power steering. Automatic headlights. Automatic wipers. Leather seats. With adjustable lumbar support! There are some buttons on the side of the seat there. Check it out, Nair. Who said crime doesn't pay?"

By the time Nair had optimised his ergonomics, Koshy had turned right. They were heading north along Chittoor Road into Edapally, the former seat of the Edapally Rajas.

"I recognise this place," Nair said, looking out the

window. "Yes. That's the Ganapati[1] Temple. One of the first places I visited when I arrived in Cochin. My mother insisted."

"Good choice," Koshy said. "You Hindus have a choice of gods. We Christians have to make do with one. Not that I'm complaining, you understand. One is hard enough. But, if I had a choice, I too would choose the Remover of Obstacles."

Koshy turned into a street lined on either side by shops selling automobile parts. Halfway down, he swung through a set of gates leading under an apartment building. The sign on the gate said "Suresh Auto Repairs".

The garage occupied half of the building's basement footprint. The other half was designated for residents' parking. Suresh's specialty seemed to be vintage Mercedes Benz cars. There were at least three in various states of disassembly, none less than twenty-five years old. Nair noticed that a white Mahindra Scorpio occupied the penultimate bay. Koshy swung in next to it and turned the ignition off. A man in a mechanic's overalls appeared at the driver's door as the two Sub-Inspectors got out. Koshy handed the man the key.

"Let's go," Koshy said to Nair. "In that car."

Mystified, Nair got into the back seat of the Scorpio with Koshy. The driver's seat was empty. The man in the front passenger seat was wearing Customs uniform whites and gold epaulettes on his shoulders. All Nair could see of him in the rear-view mirror was a pair of silvered Aviator sunglasses.

"All clear, Koshy?" the man asked, without turning.

"Yes, sir," Koshy replied. "This is Sub-Inspector Nair. Nair, this is the Deputy Commissioner of Customs."

The man nodded slightly. "Yes. We met briefly a few

moments ago. Welcome, Sub-Inspector. Good to have you on board."

"Thank you, sir," Nair replied.

"Good job," the officer said. "And I like your plan. It is unconventional, Sub-Inspector, but frankly, we'll take any option we have at the moment if it allows us to progress this case. Without politicians getting wind of what we're up to. Koshy, are you set up to start?"

Koshy nodded. "Yes, sir. Once the Audi is kitted out. That shouldn't take Suresh long."

"Excellent," the DCC said. "Bin Jamal arrives tomorrow. The two of you will be the welcoming party. The SUV will have security clearance for the VIP pickup zone at the airport. A Customs and Immigration Officer will complete the formalities without Bin Jamal having to enter the terminal. That should impress him."

"And then, sir?" Nair asked. "What do we do?"

The officer's brow furrowed. "Why, whatever he wants. Take him wherever he has to go. Play the part of lackeys. Speak only basic English. Keep your eyes and ears open. Look for any way in to Very Famous Spice House. The SUV will be wired, of course. And we'll try to tap into his phone, though that may not be easy. Or quick. He has a foreign SIM, which complicates matters."

"What if Bin Jamal's been tipped off?" Nair said. "Moopan fled to Dubai. I'm concerned he might have got in touch with Bin Jamal."

"In which case," the DCC said, "Bin Jamal will simply not show. Koshy doesn't seem to think Moopan will contact the Arab. I can't see Moopan advertising the fact that he might be a suspect in a murder case. All his business associates will drop him like a hot pakora. Moopan has too much to lose. I think he'll keep his mouth shut and hope we're not on to him. As far as he knows, we're not."

"But Moopan's driver—"

"Sequestered," the DCC replied. "The driver won't be able to communicate with anyone."

"This is a high-risk strategy, sir," Nair said. "If it goes wrong, we'll have damaged your case. For good."

The DCC grunted. "I'll live with that, Sub-Inspector. It's difficult enough to progress any high-profile investigation without some politician weighing in. We're used to having the rug pulled out from under our chappals. I'd rather we tripped ourselves up than have someone else do it."

"Inspector Kurien will expect me—" Koshy began.

The officer raised a hand. "Taken care of. I've spoken to the IG. Kurien has been told that you've been seconded to 'an important task.' Kurien did not protest, I'm told. We've had our eyes on Kurien for a while now. He's on our list, but he's a small fish. He'll have to wait."

The driver's door opened and another man in Customs whites got in.

"I need to be elsewhere, gentlemen," the DCC said. "See yourselves out, won't you? And good luck."

They watched the Scorpio drive off.

"So," Nair said, "it's on."

"Yup," said Koshy.

"We need a game plan, Koshy. Who's going to be who? I think you should be the driver, and I'll—"

"What?" Koshy glared at Nair. "What do you mean, I should be the driver? You be the driver. I'll be the, well, tour guide, or Customer Services representative, or—"

Nair shook his head. "My plan. We do it my way, Koshy. Besides, I don't drive."

Koshy looked fit to be tied. "What do you mean, you

don't drive? It's easy. Just like driving a bike, except the clutch is the left foot, not the left hand. And the gears are the left hand, not the left foot. And you don't even need to balance. Piece of cake. I'll teach you."

Koshy did. Or at least tried to. After Nair's third attempt at overtaking, Koshy leaned over from the passenger seat and grabbed the steering wheel. The SUV pulled in to the pavement. The engine juddered and died.

"What's wrong?" Nair said. "I thought I was doing fine. There was plenty of space between the bus and—"

"The other bus," Koshy said, plucking the key out of the ignition. "For a moped, Nair. Not an SUV. We were almost mincemeat."

"Nonsense," Nair replied. "The oncoming bus braked, didn't it? We got through the gap fine."

"Oh, yes," Koshy replied. "We got through it. With about two inches to spare. But what about that fellow on the scooter you cut up?"

Nair looked perturbed. He turned and glanced back through the rear window. "Scooter? What scooter?"

"Exactly," Koshy said, opening the passenger door. "Get out. I'll drive. You be whatever you want to be."

18

Abdullah Bin Jamal was used to the finer things in life. Although he came from Bedouin stock, he had never experienced the nomadic lifestyle his grandfather had spoken about. Nor did he wish to. Sleeping under the stars, eating dates and drinking camel's milk—these were not Abdullah's realities.

Abdullah's father, Mohammed, had made it big in real estate when Dubai began transforming itself into an economic powerhouse. Mohammed had seen the future; he'd borrowed against the family pearl-fishing business and snapped up a then worthless strip of land along the creek. Fifty years later, that land housed office blocks, apartments and shopping malls. Mohammed was a millionaire several times over. This meant that Abdullah, second son of the first wife, slept on Egyptian cotton, bathed twice a day and never had occasion to breathe in air that was not conditioned, filtered and humidified to exactly the right degree.

They had schooled Abdullah at a private school and

then sent him to the US for university. On return, Abdullah had been supposed to join the family firm, working under his brother, Saleh, but Abdullah rankled at playing second fiddle to anyone. It was an acquaintance of an acquaintance who had broached the idea of Abdullah joining the import-export business. With the family name behind him, capital was not a problem. And so Abdullah became Executive Vice-President of a firm that operated out of the Free Trade Zone in Jebel Ali.

Abdullah wasn't required to do much beyond deploy his influence as needed and spend his pay-check as desired, but Abdullah felt he should do more. So he took on the onerous task of visiting the firm's suppliers and customers across the world, suffering the indignities of chauffeured limousines, first-class travel, and communing with his inferiors. It was also an opportunity to leave the wives and children behind.

The captain had barely switched off the aircraft's engines before a steward appeared at his seat.

"Mr. Jamal, sir," the steward had said. "If you would care to disembark first? There is a delegation waiting for you."

Jamal grunted. The steward took that for assent, and waited while Jamal collected his laptop, his iPhone and his noise-cancelling headphones. Jamal set the *ghutra*[1] on his head and made sure the *agal*[2] was dangling the right way. Jamal preferred to dress in Western-style clothing when travelling but he found wearing the Emirati national dress, the *kandura*[3], eased his passage through Dubai airport security. The officers were all Emiratis, like himself. They saw the *kandura* and waved him on. Jamal had planned to change out of it in flight, but he had had a late night the evening before, and fallen asleep as soon as the aircraft's wheels left the ground.

Jamal felt a prickle of apprehension when he saw who awaited him. The delegation comprised two uniformed officers. Jamal's unease grew as they walked him up the jet bridge. Instead of turning left toward 'ARRIVALS', the officers used their swipe cards to open a glass door to the right. They went down a flight of stairs and through another door. Jamal found himself in front of a desk, manned by a third officer.

"Passport, please, sir," the officer said, holding his hand out.

"What is the problem?" Jamal asked, in English. "Why am I being checked like this? I am-"

The officer behind the desk smiled. "No problem at all, sir. We have been asked to expedite your passage through the airport. Standard for all VIPs. Passport. Please."

The officer gave the passport a cursory inspection, then stamped it with sufficient force to set the desk rattling. He handed it back. "Have a pleasant stay."

"This way, sir," his escort said, leading him down another corridor and through a final security door.

They were outside the terminal building in the shade of a fabric canopy, an area sequestered from the hustle and bustle of the common Arrivals area by a manned gatehouse and a security barrier. The sign above the barrier said 'VIP PICKUP AREA—AUTHORISED VEHICLES ONLY!'. There was a black Audi SUV parked nearby, engine running. The passenger door swung open. A rather tall man with a fine moustache and a matching nose got out. The man was dressed in white trousers, a white short-sleeved shirt and white socks. The shoes were brown Oxfords.

"Mr. Jamal?" said Sub-Inspector Vasanth Nair, inclining

his head and trying, against his nature, to appear servile. "Good morning. Welcome to Cochin. I am Raghavan, your Travel Experience Liaison."

Nair and Koshy had argued long and hard about names and titles on the drive to the airport. Being relegated to the driver seemed to have got Koshy's back up, and Koshy was being obstructive. Or so Nair thought.

"No," Koshy said, leaning heavily on the horn to emphasise the point. "I am not being difficult. You need to be convincing, Nair. Calling yourself 'Jason, the Customer Services Experience Manager' will not pass muster. You don't look like a Jason. He was a Greek hero. Young, flashing eyes and dark curls. He commanded a ship full of heroes. You, on the other hand, are old, irritable, and you only have one hero onboard." Koshy pointed a thumb at himself. "Me. And the only vessel you've ever managed has been that disgrace of a moped."

"Fine," Nair had said. He had no intention of calling himself 'Tour Guide', as Koshy suggested. Even if their cover was made up, there was still an operational hierarchy. And Koshy, as driver, was subordinate in the pecking order. Which is why Nair decided to call himself 'Travel Experience Liaison.' And hadn't told Koshy about his title.

Jamal looked unimpressed at Nair's introduction. Jamal held his satchel out to Nair. Nair stared at it for a moment before taking it. "This way, sir," Nair said, turning to the car.

Koshy, also in a deconstructed white Customs uniform, already had the rear passenger door and the boot open. As Nair and Bin approached the car, Koshy shouted at the porters who had just emerged from the terminal with four Louis Vuitton suitcases.

"Quickly, quickly," Koshy said in Malayalam. "Don't

damage the luggage. Or the car. Both are worth more than twelve generations of your miserable forebears! The Arabian master will want to get going. Speed up! Come on!"

Jamal slid into the rear seat without comment; he was already on his phone, speaking to someone in loud Arabic. Nair closed the door, then placed Jamal's satchel on top of the rest of the luggage in the boot. Koshy swung the lid down without warning, Nair leaping out of the way just in time.

Nair glowered at Koshy. "Listen, Koshy—"

"Hey!" Koshy hissed at Nair in Malayalam. "No real names, buffoon. This is an undercover operation. Use my alias."

Nair scowled. "Fine. Get in the car. Let's get going. Driver." He didn't wait for Koshy's reply.

They had just turned left out of the airport when their passenger spoke for the first time. Jamal had a deep, gravelly voice.

"What is your name?"

Nair half-turned. Jamal was pointing at him.

"Raghavan, sir." Nair said. "I am the Travel Experience Liaison for—"

Jamal waved him to silence. "Rag? Haven?"

"Raghavan. It's pronounced 'rug' 'heaven'."

"Rag? Haven?" Jamal tried it out, then shook his head. "Too complicated. Indian names too complicated. You should have something simple. Like Abdullah. Or Mutawassib. No, you, I will call 'Rag'." He clicked his fingers and pointed at Koshy. "That one. His name?"

Nair's jaw dropped. They hadn't discussed what Koshy would call himself. No one ever addressed drivers by anything except the term 'driver.'

"He is the driver, sir." Nair said.

Jamal clicked his fingers again. "That I can see. Name? Name?"

"Madhavan." Koshy said with finality. "Madhavan is my name, sir."

Jamal frowned. "Mad? Haven? Also, too complicated. No, no, no, no, no." He pointed at Koshy. "You, I will call 'Mad'. Mad and Rag. Yes, that will do. You know where to go?"

Nair blanched. "No, we were just told to pick you up—"

Jamal nodded. "Good. You should not know. Security. Now, I will tell you. The Vemba-Vumba-Vomba, ya Allah, another complicated word." Jamal turned his phone towards Nair. "This hotel here. On this island. Bol—bol—bol—what is this word?"

Koshy glanced over his shoulder at the screen. He spoke, in English, before Nair could answer. "The Grand Vembanad Hotel, sir. On Bolghatty island. Bolghatty Island is where the royal palace of the Cochin royal family is located. It is a—"

Nair interrupted, speaking to Koshy in Malayalam. "Shut up, Mad. Drivers are supposed to drive, not talk to the clients. I will do the talking." Nair turned to Jamal and spoke in English. "Yes, sir, as Mad was saying, it is where the Cochin royal family palace used to be. It's a very nice hotel, very luxurious, full of all the luxuries. Several. Like a swimming pool, um, also a tennis court, no, two tennis courts, rooftop bar. Or is that a poolside bar? Both. Yes, there's both—"

Nair might have carried on in this vein if Jamal hadn't gone back to scrolling through his phone, ignoring Nair's narrative completely.

Koshy smirked, replying under his breath in Malayalam. "Probably better if you don't talk too much either, Rag. There's no tennis court. There's a squash court and a gymnasium. Two swimming pools. And a rooftop infinity pool. And four bars, including poolside. Though I don't think our Muslim client will be that interested in the alcohol."

The rest of the drive passed in uncompanionable silence at the front and lots more loud Arabic in the back. The two Sub-Inspectors only spoke again once they had offloaded their cargo at the Grand Vembanad.

The SUV had barely come to a stop in the hotel's driveway before a flock of uniformed porters descended on the vehicle, like carrion onto still-quivering roadkill. Nair got out, but the doorman beat him to Jamal's door, ushering the Arab out with bows and smiles into the care of a uniformed concierge. The concierge wielded an oversized umbrella patterned in the style of those borne by elephants during the famous *Trishur puram*[4] festival.

Nair watched the procession ascend up the steps and disappear through the doors. Koshy joined him.

"What now?" Nair said. "Do we wait? Or leave? Maybe I should go ask him."

Koshy shook his head. "That's the problem with you upper caste landlord landowner feudal types. You're used to people waiting for you. Now, at this other end of the socio-economic spectrum, Rag, when you're the one doing the waiting, you do just that. You. Wait. Until the master reappears. Or sends instructions."

The doorman waved them on to the parking area at the rear. With the sun high in the sky, Koshy found a spot in the shade of a coconut palm, and turned the ignition off.

"What is it with us Indians?" Nair asked no one in

particular. "One foreigner shows up and everyone bows and scrapes. It's as if we were still an Imperial colony."

Koshy snorted. "And why not? It's not as if the Indian customers are any more generous to their inferior countrymen than visiting foreigners. When you're a porter, or a doorman, all you can expect from your high-brow Indian customers is casual disregard. Might as well bow and scrape a bit more for the foreigners, who might hand you a ten-dollar note in passing. I mean, I don't see you treating your Indian subordinates like your equals. Do you?"

Nair bristled. "That's different. That's-"

"Exactly the same thing," Koshy said. "Except you call it caste. Or rank. Or hierarchy. Am I wrong?" Koshy adjusted his seat until he was reclining just short of horizontal. "Anyway, I'll leave you to consider that matter deeply. I'm going to have a nap."

Nair was still constructing his riposte twenty minutes later when there was a knock at the window. It was the concierge. He waved for the window to be lowered.

"Your boss wants you to be ready to leave in ten minutes. Start the engine. Get the air-conditioner going. Then swing round to the front." The concierge turned to go.

"Where?" Nair said, as he shook Koshy awake with a hand on Koshy's shoulder. "Where are we going?"

The concierge looked puzzled. "A sari shop. That's what he said."

It was Nair's turn to look puzzled. "Sari shop? But he didn't bring his wife. Who's the sari for?"

The concierge shrugged. "Maybe it's for his mistress." An evil grin appeared on his face. "Or maybe the Arab enjoys dressing up in saris at night, when he's all alone. Who cares? Just be ready."

Koshy raised his seat and started the engine. "Bloody hell. Sari shopping. My second worst kind of hell."

Nair raised an eyebrow. "Oh? What's the first?"

Koshy shifted into reverse and looked over his shoulder. "Hang around, Nair, and you might just find out."

19

Smiley Silks was very much the fabric upstart on Mahatma Gandhi Road. The premises used to be an office building for an international bank. A group of investors had bought the building and repurposed into what they termed "the premier sari destination in India". It was no coincidence that Smiley Silks' neighbour was Verma's Textile Emporium, the oldest and, until that point, the most prestigious sari shop in the city.

Verma's had, for forty years, operated out of a traditional single-storey brick bungalow, with a pitched tile roof and a verandah. The sign above the entrance was hand-painted and fading. There was no air-conditioning, only ceiling fans. Patrons browsed the offerings seated on mats on the floor, while their drivers double-parked on the buzzing thoroughfare outside. It was the traditional way of doing things and customers came to Verma's because tradition carried value.

Smiley Silks strove to be different. It sprawled over four floors, the bottom three dedicated to saris. Instead of a sign, they erected a video screen the size of a tennis court that displayed nubile young models in constant motion. The entire building was centrally air-conditioned. There was valet parking and complimentary drinks (including smoothies) for their clientele. And no one sat on the floor. Smiley Silks gave tradition a proper poke in the eye.

The old guard paid the upstart no mind. “A fad,” they said to each other, “it’ll never catch on. The old ways are best.” And so they turned their backs, while their old clientele died out, and the young flocked to Smiley’s in their droves.

Koshy glared out the window at the valet and sent him packing with a muttered curse. Nair already had Jamal’s door open—Nair was learning that the super-rich brooked no delay. Jamal emerged, dressed in designer denim and a Versace shirt. The Arab had abandoned his traditional dress and now looked, for all the world, like any other ageing hipster.

“Rag, you wait,” Jamal said, striding off towards the entrance.

“I presume that means Mad too,” Koshy called out to Nair, in Malayalam. “What an ass. I can’t wait until we have him locked up. I’ll show him what Mad is all about.” Koshy winked at Nair. “I might even ‘lose the Rag’, so to speak.”

Nair ignored Koshy. Nair was watching Jamal like a hawk.

“What’s going on here?” Nair said. “That idiot has just accosted the doorman. Now he’s taking his wallet out. Money? Odd. He’s tipped no one so far. He’s waving something. Looks like a card. A gold card.”

Koshy joined Nair in front of the bonnet. “Credit card? Maybe it’s one of those super-premium cards.” Koshy caught Nair’s puzzled look. “You know, free airport lounge access, someone to pick up your laundry, discounts on luxury goods. What? What's wrong with you?"

Nair's brow furrowed. "Why would you need someone to pick up your laundry? And where from? The dhobi[1] collects. And delivers."

Koshy looked up to heaven. "Peasant. I need to educate you in the ways of the world, Nair. Just you wait. Once this case is over—"

Koshy was speaking to empty air. Nair was gone. He was ascending the same steps Jamal had just ascended, angling for the doorman.

"Oh, bloody hell!" Koshy said, starting after Nair at a trot. Parts of him moved out of sync with other, firmer parts. Koshy resolved to lay off the ethakkappams.

By the time Koshy had reached the foot of the steps, Nair was making his way back down.

"Where is he?" Koshy asked, scanning the shopfront. "Where did he go?"

Nair gestured with his head. "Around the corner. There's a separate entrance at the side. Come on, let's get back to the car." Nair filled Koshy in as they walked back across the parking lot. "Apparently there's a private lounge for gentlemen companions of wives and daughters. Somewhere for men to relax and while away the hours while their female family members wile away the bank account. That's where he's gone."

The valet was waiting for them in front of the SUV.

"Hey!" he said, rather rudely. "Can't park here. There are other customers arriving. Move it on. Around the side." He gestured with one hand, then turned and walked off.

"Sorry!" Koshy said to the man's back. "I didn't realise your grandfather owned the place."

'Around the side' turned out to be a lane between the

building itself and the boundary wall, already full of parked vehicles. Koshy brought the car to a stop as Nair lowered the window and peered out.

"Yes," Nair said, "it's there. Look."

There was a rather plain door set in the side wall of the complex, half-hidden from view by a strategic deployment of potted palms and topiary. Above the door was a jolly silk canopy in red and yellow. There was a plaque next to the door that read

'GENTLEMEN'S RELAXATION LOUNGE
★ PATRONS ONLY ★
ADMISSION AT MANAGEMENT DISCRETION.'

A pair of dangerous-looking Nepalese security men in charcoal grey uniforms guarded the door.

Koshy peered out. "Well, there's no way we're getting in there. Just as well. What now? There isn't a single free parking bay here. What do we do? Just go round and round the building?"

Nair looked around. Just ahead stood another sign that read "Underground Parking↘". Nair pointed. "That way. Go down. We'll figure it out."

Koshy took the turn, and they descended into the concrete bowels of Smiley Silks. Koshy parked the Audi between two concrete pillars.

"Something odd about this lounge," Nair said. "It's supposed to be patrons only. But Jamal didn't go into the store to buy anything. And he doesn't have a wife here spending his money. Yet he got in."

Koshy nodded. "You're right. Maybe it's a cover. Maybe he's meeting a contact there. Great place for shady business deals."

Nair had that dogged look on his face, like a hungry eagle spotting a marmoset. "We need to get in there, Koshy. We need to find out what's going on."

"No, no, no, no, no." Koshy wagged a metronomic finger. "The DCC said watch, not enter. We're supposed to be reconnaissance, not infiltration. Collect data. Observe. Let's just scope out the—oh, hell!"

Nair had left again, the slam of the passenger door signalling his departure.

By the time Koshy found Nair, the Sub-Inspector was looming over the solitary parking attendant. The attendant had been dozing on his aluminium chair against a concrete pillar. The man sprung to his feet as Nair prodded him in the shoulder.

"You can go that way, sir," the attendant said, pointing with one hand and wiping sleep away from his eyes with the other. "There is a lift there." He grinned shyly, as if afraid to say more. "But customers only."

"We are customers, fellow," Nair replied. "This is my driver. My wife is shopping up there. I heard there is a lounge for men. To wait."

The attendant wagged his head and tugged at his drab grey uniform. "Oh, sorry, sir. I should have known from your manner. Of course, you are a Sir. And that man is your driver? Of course. Lift will take you to the Relaxation Lounge, sir. Just press the 'R' button."

Nair nodded and walked off. "Give the man something, Madhavan," he called back over his shoulder. Koshy gave Nair's back a glare, then fished out a crumpled note which he threw at the attendant. Koshy caught up with Nair at the elevator door.

"This is a terrible idea, Nair! If Jamal catches us, we're

screwed. And there's no back-up. What if we're taken hostage? Or beaten? Or shot?"

Nair glanced sidelong at Koshy as the lift door opened. "Sh! CCTV camera in the lift. Just play along. We'll be fine." With that, Nair stepped into the lift and crossed his arms, waiting for Koshy to follow.

Seeing no other choice, Koshy stepped through the closing doors. He cast a quick peek upward; in the corner was a black glass orb peering at them.

"Well?" Nair said, loudly. "What are you waiting for, driver? Press the button. Do I have to do everything myself? Better be careful. Carry on like this and I'll send you back!"

Koshy gritted his teeth. "Sorry. Sir." He jabbed at the button, imagining it was Vasanth Nair's left eye.

The elevator spoke to them in an upmarket woman's voice.

"You have selected. Floor R. Please stand clear of the doors."

20

Floor R was at the very top of the building. The elevator rose at speed past floors G, 1 and 2, coming to a stop with another exhortation.

"Relaxation Lounge. Doors opening. Have a nice day."

The elevator doors slid open to a scene neither police officer had ever beheld. They were standing on the threshold of an open-plan lounge, subdivided by carved sandalwood partitions into intimate nooks. Each alcove contained low leather armchairs and glass coffee-tables. Freestanding brass floor lamps created islands of light. A single ornamental light fixture hung in the air, itself composed of hundreds of glittering orbs tinted ruby red and brilliant emerald green. Luxurious deep-pile carpet covered the floor. The textured wallpaper depicted hunting scenes from old Mughal tapestries. The air was pleasantly cool and scented with jasmine. Smooth jazz played in the background, under the clink of cutlery and the murmur of muted conversation.

There was a reception desk beside the entryway. It was

unattended. Nair and Koshy stepped out of the lift. The doors hissed shut behind them.

"What now?" Koshy whispered. "I hope you have a plan, Nair!"

"Shut up!" Nair hissed back. "I don't. But something will come. Just follow my lead."

"Good afternoon, sirs!" A young woman approached. She was about shoulder height with a fair complexion and long dark hair tied in a bun behind her head. She wore charcoal trousers and a matching waistcoat over a cream blouse. "Welcome to the Relaxation Lounge. Do you have a reservation? May I have your names, please?"

Nair stepped forward. "Yes. We are with one of your guests. He's already here, I believe. Mr. Jamal. An Arabian gentleman."

The woman nodded and stepped up to the desk. Her name badge read 'Nandita | Guest Relations'.

"Just a moment, sir." She tapped at a keyboard. "Ah, yes. A group booking, I see. And yes, the gentleman in question has already arrived. You are Mr. Moopan? Welcome, sir. It is a pleasure to have you." She smiled at Nair, displaying perfect white teeth.

Nair didn't miss a beat. "Yes. Good to be here. Yes. Very good. Is Mr. Jamal, um, occupied? In relaxation?"

"Oh, yes," Nandita said. "He didn't wish to wait, Mr. Moopan. I see you have booked the Silk Package for Mr. Jamal and yourself. That includes the full Relaxation Treatment and a private lounge afterwards, with complimentary access to the bar and our hot buffet. The Silk Package comes with butler service, sir. No need to go to the buffet yourself." She frowned, glancing over Nair's shoulder at Koshy, before looking down at her screen again. "Only the booking is only for two people?"

Nair glanced over his shoulder at Koshy.

"Ah, yes," Nair said, slowly. "This is Madhavan. He is my dr—"

"Director of Operations," Koshy said, in a cut-glass English accent. "So pleased to meet you, Nandita. It was my very own Personal Assistant that made the booking. Yes. I hadn't planned on being here, but I rearranged my extremely busy calendar. If you can accommodate myself, that would be most conducive to a fruitful and productive collaboration." Koshy ended with a cheesy grin.

Nair raised an eyebrow. Nandita spoke before Nair could reply.

"Of course, sir. Mr. Madhavan, we would be only too thrilled to have you with us. Let me see what is available." She tapped at the keyboard. Her face fell. "Ah, unfortunately, the only package we have available at the moment is our Chiffon package. It doesn't have the full Relaxation Spa Treatments as the Silk package, but we can upgrade all the post-Relaxation facilities for no charge. With our compliments." She looked up. "It would be our honour to accommodate you both, as regular and valued clients of our Relaxation Lounge."

Nair frowned. "Well, I don't think that's necessary, really. Madhavan—"

"Would be pleased to accept," Koshy replied, stepping forward. "As a regular and valued client."

"Thank you, sir," Nandita said. "Any particular requirements? Or requests?"

Nair considered this. Koshy answered.

"Well, Mr. Moopan there is vegetarian. Though he eats fish. As for me?" Koshy grinned again. "Nothing is off limits."

"I'll just make a note," Nandita said. "I'm pleased to say

our Relaxation Treatments are 100% vegetarian and vegan-friendly. They're also gluten-free. If the gentlemen will follow me?"

She led them through the archway into the lounge. Nair checked out the patrons as they passed: all middle-aged paunchy men of wealth. They lounged in armchairs, reading newspapers or drinking. Some were perusing the hot buffet, a splendid selection of sweet and savoury dishes set out on silver chafing dishes, attended by servers in uniform.

Nandita led them to an ornate teak door in the far wall. She touched a proximity card to the keypad on the wall and the door unlocked. She held it open for them. They were in a wood-panelled corridor. The lighting was altogether more subtle, cast by wall-mounted sconces. The music was a low-tempo groove with a meandering bass-line.

"This way, sirs," she said, following. "Mr. Madhavan, your experience is here, on your left."

She stopped at the first door. This had a framed strip of scarlet fabric set into the woodwork at head height. The word "CHIFFON" was emblazoned in a flowing script. She unlocked the door with another tap of the card, opened it and gestured to Koshy that he should enter.

Koshy gave Nair a backward glance, then stepped through. Nandita closed the door behind him.

"I hope Madhavan will be alright," Nair said, falling into step behind her. "He's not used to the luxuries in life, you know. A hard worker. Hardly any time to relax."

"I'm sure he will be fine, sir," Nandita replied with a giggle. "All of our customers emerge entirely relaxed after their treatments. And please don't worry. Our therapists can be as gentle or as vigorous as the client wishes."

The last set of doors faced each other at the end of the

corridor. Both had a fabric swatch that said "SILK". Nandita unlocked the door on the left.

"There you are, Mr. Moopan. Your therapist will be with you directly. Please, make yourself comfortable."

"Thanks," Nair said. He pointed at the other door. "I take it Mr. Jamal is in there?"

Nandita inclined her head in agreement. "Yes. I will let the gentleman know you have arrived once he has completed his treatment. Please enjoy yourself."

With that, she closed the door on him.

Nair spun around to take in what the Silk Relaxation Treatment Area looked like. It was not what he expected.

21

Nair had expected a massage table, perhaps a hot tub or even a sauna. This room had none of the accoutrements of such therapy. It looked, for all purposes, like an upmarket hotel room.

There was an enormous bed in the centre, a dressing table, a velvet *chaise longue*, coir carpet underfoot and a very glittery light fixture hanging down from the ceiling. The air carried just a hint of sandalwood. A single pane of glass formed the far wall, tinted almost to blackness, through which Nair could see nothing of the outside world. There were two other doors, both closed, one he presumed to be the toilet and the other the wardrobe.

He'd never been to a spa before. The nearest approximation in Nair's experience had been the traditional '*chavutti thirumal*[1]' massage. That had taken place on an austere Ayurvedic retreat, in a brick-walled room with mats on the floor and a pair of ropes hanging from the ceiling. Nair had lain on the mats while the masseur, holding on to the ropes, walked all over him. Nair had emerged refreshed, if somewhat concerned about the condition of the masseur's corns.

There were no mats in this room. There were ropes, but these were braided black leather, dangling from a square wooden frame screwed to a wall. A long ebony box stood at the very foot of the frame.

Nair walked over and lifted the lid of the box. Inside he found implements the like of which he had never seen before. Some he understood the purpose of. The black blindfold was clearly to facilitate a good night's sleep, though why one would need such a thing in this room was beyond him. With the lights off, the room would certainly be in total darkness, thanks to the tinted window. The tasselled thing with the ebony handle was a feather duster of some sort, but very impractical, he thought; the tassels were black leather, and rough. Any dusting done with that was likely to damage the furniture, such was its heft. He couldn't figure out why there were handcuffs in the box. Or a whip. Or a dog's collar, studded with spikes.

He might have considered the mystery further if he hadn't heard the snick of a latch. He turned around and saw the wardrobe door open. What stepped out fixed Nair to the spot. The only word he could summon to describe the vision before him was *apsara*[2].

The woman was young and short. As she turned to close the door behind her, Nair saw a braid of long black hair lying against her back. She wore a backless blouse, the skin between her shoulder blades glistening. Her feet were bare and her ankles, beneath an embroidered scarlet *ghagra*[3], were encircled by anklets with tiny bells on them. They jangled as she glided across the floor towards him.

Nair retreated. She matched his every step until his back was against the window and she was barely a foot away.

Large dark eyes looked into his. Beneath a tiny nose, her mouth was wide, the lips cherry red. She smiled, revealing tiny, white teeth. She brought her hands up in a namaste, her palms meeting before the immodest expanse of cleavage. There was much cleavage. Nair averted his eyes.

"Good afternoon, sir," she said in a throaty voice. "Please. Call me Silk. I am here for your total relaxation and enjoyment. My mission is your satisfaction." The last word flowed out, rippling with sibilance.

Nair sought appropriate words, but his mind was blank. He tried his voice instead, but his vocal cords seemed to have left the country. He could only stare as she took another step forward. She tilted her head up and spoke again, her breath fresh and scented with cinnamon.

"Sir is nervous?" There was mischief in her voice. She placed a hand on his chest, a hot, dry hand. She giggled. "Why! Sir's heart is racing! Like a tabla!" Her fingers played over his chest. She sighed. "Silk will soothe all your worries."

Her nimble fingers were at his shirt buttons. She had undone two before Nair regained control over his muscles.

"What?" was all he could manage at first. "Who?" followed, as if afraid to be left behind. "How?" trotted after, unwilling to be the lone thought left in Nair's brain.

She giggled again. "Oh, Sir is curious." She was on the third button now. "Who I am, I have told you already. My name is Silk. You can call me Silk or Silky or Aparna or Hema or any name you like. Actress. Secretary. Sister-in-law. Sir decides." She leaned in close. "What and how? Well, that is up to you. Sir."

It was as if she had eight arms. Whenever Nair detached her hands from his person, another hand seemed to attach itself to him somewhere else. Fend her off the buttons and she was at his belt. Pull a hand away from that and she was at the buttons again. Shirtsleeve, collar, pockets—no part of him was off-limits, it seemed. He shook her off and ran for the door to the corridor. He wrenched at the handle, but it did not move.

He spun around, his back to the wood. She advanced upon him, a pair of handcuffs in her hand. The chain clinked in time with the jangling of the bells.

"Some Sirs prefer Silk to take control. Maybe this Sir is one of those? Hmm?" She shook the handcuffs. "If you wish, I can cuff you. Then I can tie you up, Sir. Then," she paused, "I can beat you." She ran forward and pressed herself against him. Her chest heaved against his. Nair stared at her, eyes wide. He felt something cool encircle one wrist. There was a click as the handcuff closed. "I think you'd like that, Sir. I think you'd like that very much."

As she reached for his unshackled wrist, his mother's words rang in Nair's ears.

"First, meat. Then, liquor. Then, women. The steps leading down into Hell. Be careful, Vasanth. Be very careful!"

It was far too late for caution.

22

Five minutes later, Sub-Inspector Nair had regained the upper hand. As Silk brought Nair's free wrist towards the open handcuff, Nair's brain had woken up. Nair grabbed the girl's wrists and spun her around. She did not resist. She crashed back against his chest, landing with an exhilarated gasp.

"Oh, Sir!" she said. "Now you are taking control! Silk likes men who know what they want!"

Nair did not reply. He wrapped his arms around her stomach and hoisted her into the air. He staggered over to the bed, Silk's delighted squeals sounding with every step. With a grunt, he threw her onto the mattress. She landed gracefully, scrambling over onto her back. She stared up at him, her lips parted. Her chest rose and fell with every breath.

"Why, Sir—" she said. "You are so strong!"

"Silence!" Nair raised an imperious finger, the effect diminished somewhat by the handcuffs dangling from that wrist. "Silence, woman!"

Her eyes grew. She giggled again. "Yes, Sir," she said, in

a meek voice. She lowered her head. "I will obey your commands. Sir!"

"Listen to me! I am a police officer!"

She glanced up at him. She bit her lower lip. "Yes, Mr. Police Officer. What have I done wrong? Is my dress too short?" She reached down and slid the skirt up her ankles. "Oh, I have been such a naughty girl!"

Nair glared at her. "No! I am! I really am a police officer! Sub-Inspector Nair!"

The skirt had ridden up her shins. "Oh, I know," she cooed. "Everyone fears the Big Bad Police Inspector." She blinked at him. "Am I—am I going to be punished, Inspector Nair? Please punish me. Don't send me to Big Bad Jail!"

Both kneecaps were now revealed. The skirt's perilous ascent continued.

Nair clapped one hand over his eyes, took a glancing blow from the dangling handcuff and fished in his pocket with the other hand. He held his police ID out, eyes still closed.

"No, you idiot woman! I AM a Police Inspector! Look! This is my ID!"

Silence. He peeked out between his fingers. He had deployed his ID just in time. A few more inches and all modesty would have abandoned.

Silk was peering at the ID. Her eyes widened again. Her jaw dropped.

"Police?" she gasped in horror. "You are—police?"

Nair let fall the hand covering his eyes.

"Yes, you *rakshasi*[1]! Lower that skirt immediately! What's wrong with you? Get up off that bed! Now. You are under arrest. Right after you find the keys to these bloody handcuffs!"

Nair unlocked the handcuffs while the girl cowered on the bed. She had retreated to the headboard, huddled there with a pillow clutched to her chest. She was sobbing gently, her head lowered.

"Stop that!" Nair said. She started, glanced up. "Stop! Now!" She wiped her nose with the back of one hand and nodded.

"Sir! I am sorry, sir!" Her voice was pleading. "I-I didn't know! Sir, I just work here. I just do what I am told to do, sir! I didn't know—"

Nair raised a hand. "Silence! No talking, woman. You will answer my questions. Now. Tell the truth. Or else!"

It didn't take long. Relaxation Club was a high-class brothel. Silk's real name was Amba. She was from Rajasthan, in the far north of India. Her family, poor tenant farmers, had sold her off as a child to pay off her father's debts to the landowner. She'd worked as a servant in her owner's household until she came of age, at which point she'd been sold on again to work in a brothel. Two years ago, she'd been brought to Cochin. She didn't know how old she was because she didn't know her birthday. She didn't know the name of the village she came from. Yes, there were other girls working here. They came from all over: Nepal, Orissa, Sri Lanka, Tamil Nadu. They all lived together in a single room on an upper floor. No, they had never been out of the building.

"It is not so bad, sir," Amba said. She'd relaxed a little. She sat on the bed with her legs crossed, the pillow across her knees. "Here, they do not beat us. And we get given some money which we can keep. They tell us that, if we do a good job and please the customers, then someday they will send us home. Maybe, with some money, I can go back to Rajasthan. Or anywhere. I don't mind. Somewhere where

I can live a good life." She smiled shyly at him. "I want to open a shop. An embroidery shop, sir. I can do embroidery very well. I learned it from other girls in the house in Rajasthan. A small shop, nothing very grand. Just enough to have a home and earn a living." She lowered her head. "In some other way."

Nair sat on the chaise longue. The story had appalled him. He'd been aware of human trafficking, of course, but it was not a crime that the Mattancherry Police had ever dealt with. Such matters were the province of the Vice Squad.

Amba glanced up at him again. "Sir? Will it be a long sentence in jail? How many years, sir? This many?" She held up one hand, fingers outstretched. "Or this many?" She raised the other hand. "Or more?" Her lip quivered. "Whatever Sir says, I will do, but I would just like to know. Please?"

Her eyes were on Nair as he got to his feet.

"None of that, now," Nair said. "You won't go to jail. I'll see to that." There was wonder in her face. He forestalled another question. "First, you need to help me. How do I get out of here?"

The door to the corridor was always locked, Amba said, in case the girl tried to escape. They only opened it at the end of the allotted time.

"But," she said, "there is another way." She looked worried.

"Go on," Nair said. "What other way?"

"There is a button, sir. There." She pointed to the dressing table. "Underneath. In case the customer gets violent. Or passes out. Sometimes, they drink too much or take things and have a fit. Only..."

"Only?"

"Only it will bring Manager Madam." She stared at him. "They will know. About you!"

Nair nodded. "Oh, will they? Good. It's about time. On your feet, girl. Press the bloody button. Look like the innocent flower, but be the serpent under it."

Amba looked confused. "Sir? Flower? Snake?"

He waved her to her feet. "Shakespeare, dear child, Shakespeare. Never mind. I will introduce you to The Immortal Bard later. On to it, now. Give me three minutes, then press the button. Then, cry havoc and let slip the dogs of war!"

The Dog of War crouched in the narrow dressing room that he had taken for a wardrobe, his ear pressed firmly against the door. He heard Amba's voice from the other side.

"Sir! I have pressed the button. I will now hide."

He heard her anklets jangle away, then silence. It took eighty-four seconds by his watch. First, there was the muffled sound of voices. Then the click of the lock. Then a creak as a door swung open. More voices, clearer now. A woman and a man. Quick footsteps scratching across the coir carpet. Passing the door. A strident male voice rang out.

"Amba! Where the bloody hell are you? And where is—"

That was all the cue that Nair needed. He tapped his pocket and heard the tinkle of the handcuffs, twisted the handle of the whip once for good measure, said a prayer to Shiva, The God of Destruction, took a breath, then emerged.

23

The man who had been doing the shouting was a tall, hefty fellow with bottlebrush eyebrows, kitted out in a grey waistcoat and cream bow tie. His head swung around as Nair stepped out. Nair saw the man's mouth flop open. The man's arms rose instinctively to cover his head.

The whip snapped down. Nair delivered the blow like a pace bowler, overhand, with his shoulder fully engaged. The man's roar of pain drowned out the crack of the strike. Nair followed through with his shoulder, sending Mr. Bow Tie flying. The man rolled across the bed in a flurry of limbs, slid off the far end, and smashed into the far corner.

The woman took two steps back. She was in her fifties and dressed in a formal sari in the same uniform colours as her fallen companion. She opened her mouth to scream, but Nair gave her a backhand slap that sent her, too, to the floor. Nair stepped over her and walked towards Mr. Bow Tie.

The man was struggling to his feet, using the wall for

leverage. His eyes rose to Nair's face. His hand rose to ward off the next blow.

"No!" the man began. "No!"

Nair kicked him in the knee. Bow Tie fell forward onto his face. Nair side-stepped to avoid the flailing arms. The Sub-Inspector leant down, stuck a knee between the man's shoulder-blades and gathered up his limp arms behind his back. The handcuffs clicked closed.

The woman was screaming now. She was on the carpet, sari in disarray, crawling towards the front door. Her shrieks were ear-piercing.

"Help! Help! Joncy! Jibu! Naveen! Anyone! Help!"

Nair leapt over her, putting himself between her and her escape route. She fell silent, her mouth open mid-scream. Her eyes rose.

"Ssh!" Nair said, touching the handle of the whip to his lips. "Shut up, idiot, or you'll get some of this!"

The bathroom door clicked open. A pair of wide eyes peered out. Nair waved at Amba.

"Come out, woman! Get some more handcuffs. Put them on this idiot here. Then strip the pillowcases off. Quickly, now!"

Once secured, Nair hauled both captives to their feet and walked them into the bathroom. Nair sat them both in the bathtub, back to back. He handed the whip to Amba.

"If any of them make a move, beat the living blood out of them. You have permission. Police permission. Understand?"

Amba tested the whip against the tile. "Yes, sir!" she said.

Nair addressed his captives. "Listen, you nitwits! I am Sub-Inspector Vasanth Nair, Cochin Police. You are both under arrest. Any attempt to move and this girl has my authority to rip the hides off your miserable backs. Understand?"

Neither captive said a word. It was difficult to talk with a pillowcase stuffed in one's mouth.

Nair walked back out into the bedroom. He picked up what Manager Madam had dropped in her panic. A keychain with a bunch of keys and a proximity card. One card to rule them all.

Nair stepped out into the corridor, closing the door softly behind him. There was no sign of Joncy, or Jibu, or even Naveen. Amba had told him that the rooms were sound-proofed. Manager Madam's screams had been in vain.

Nair retraced their route of entry until he was outside "CHIFFON". He tapped the card against the pad and shouldered the door open.

Nair had been worried about Koshy. He imagined what indignities Koshy might be suffering. Koshy was overweight and flabby—a small girl could overpower him. Nair, on the other hand, had spent some of his youth training in *kalaripayattu*[1]. Nair was far from expert, but an overweight waiter and a brothel madam were well within his powers.

As the door swung open, Nair prepared himself to liberate his colleague. Nair had expected to find the Sub-Inspector in his underwear, strapped to the wall and being worked over with a flail. Koshy, however, didn't look like he wanted to be liberated.

Koshy was in his underwear—that much was as per Nair's expectations. The underwear was a pair of once white Y-fronts. Koshy was on his front on the bed, head on a pillow, arms crossed underneath. Koshy's face was turned towards the door, his eyes closed.

A girl, dressed similarly to Amba, sat on Koshy's back,

her legs straddling his flanks. Her hands were slick with oil, oil that she rubbed onto the Sub-Inspector's back. Her forearm muscles rippled as she pressed and kneaded.

Koshy's eyes flicked open as the door bounced off the wall. Koshy jerked upright, sending the girl flying backwards. She crashed to the floor with a squeal.

"Nair!" Koshy grabbed the pillow and covered his nether regions with it. "Nair! I was—"

"Shut up, you immoral idiot! Shut up and get your trousers on! And follow me! To the other Silk room! Jamal! We have to get Jamal!"

It was an oily and shirtless Sub-Inspector Koshy that joined Nair thirty seconds later. Nair was already crouched at the door, ear to the wood. Koshy jiggled as he padded to a stop. Close up, the smell of coconut oil was overpowering.

"Ready?" Nair said.

"Nair," Koshy began, "I was only—"

Nair's reply was a hiss. "Shush, you buffoon. You can apologise later. Are you ready?"

"My shirt," Koshy said, holding it up. "Do I have time to put on—"

"No!" Nair said. "Get ready. We're going in." Nair touched the card to the reader. The door clicked. Nair nodded at Koshy.

Koshy gulped, reached for the handle and pushed the door open.

"Police!" Nair charged into the room. "Cochin Police! Hands up!"

Of the three occupants in the room, two obeyed straight away. The two young women were of a height, barely five feet tall. One was dark-skinned with long black hair, the other olive-complexioned with light brown eyes. Both wore knee-length black leather boots, leather corsets and bustiers. They dropped what they had in their hands and stepped back.

The third occupant would have obeyed if he could, but Abdullah Bin Jamal was in no position to move. Nair supposed it would be quite difficult if one were hog-tied, lying on one's front with one's bare buttocks facing the ceiling. Said buttocks were purple, presumably from the attention of the leather batons now lying on the carpet.

Nair felt more than heard Koshy pad into the room.

"What the hell—" Koshy began.

Nair silenced him with a raised hand. "Have you got your phone on you?"

"Yes," Koshy said. "It's a bit oily, but yes. Why?"

"Evidence," Nair said. "I think we need to collect some evidence."

It was then that Abdullah Bin Jamal began shouting. In Arabic. Nair couldn't understand it, but it didn't sound like a cry for help. The shouting got louder as Koshy raised his phone.

Nair stepped out of Koshy's way. And closed the door.

24

The news broke later that evening. They watched it from the Debrief Room at Customs House. The Office of the Commissioner of Customs occupied a prime location on the point of Fort Cochin Island. The view from the second floor took in the great sweep of harbour, from the Laccadive Sea to the west, across the Vembanad Lake to the twinkling lights of the city to the east. There was a squall coming in from the sea and the pleasure boats were steaming shoreward, their running lights bobbing across the water like crimson fireflies.

Customs House had a resident chef (Customs Officers keep strange hours) and Nair and Koshy had had the first meal of the day seated around the conference table while they awaited the Deputy Commissioner. The wall-mounted TV was on and the news report flashed up just as they finished eating. Koshy turned the sound up in time to catch the end of it.

The reporter was a youth with too little hair product for a coming storm—his hair whipped about his head as if it was sentient and wished to leave. Behind him, the parking lot of Smiley Silks was devoid of high-end vehicles—there wasn't a parking valet in sight. Instead, the compound looked like a police garage, so full was it with police vehicles. A pair of police constables waving *lathis*[1] forced the crowds back onto the road as their colleagues set up barriers.

> "—developments here from MG Road in Cochin. A heavy police presence has been established around the most prestigious luxury sari shop in the city. Yes, Smiley Silks is under lock-down. The shop is closed and staff have been sent home. One staff member told us how police questioned her and took her details before allowing her to leave. We don't as yet have any information about what the reason is for the police presence, but several individuals were brought out of the building and put into the back of police vans, all with their faces covered. For the moment, all we can say is that if you need to buy a wedding sari, you'd better look elsewhere. K. Vinesh, reporter, with cameraman Madhu, reporting. Back to Vimala in the studio."

THE DOOR OPENED, and two men entered. One was the Deputy Commissioner, the other a younger man with steel-framed glasses. Both wore Customs whites. Nair and Koshy got to their feet and saluted. The Deputy Commissioner waved them back down.

"Sit. Sit." The DCCC glanced at the TV screen. "I see the story's out. That didn't take long. Vijay, turn that thing off, will you?" The DCCC removed his hat, took a seat himself and pointed at the screen. "So. As I recall, that was not part of the plan. Was it? Or is my memory failing me?"

Nair looked at Koshy. Koshy looked back at Nair. Nair answered.

"No, sir. However, we were in a tight fix and we made an executive decision to—"

"We?" the DCC asked. "We? Or you, Sub-Inspector Nair?"

Nair fell silent. Koshy leapt in.

"Sub-Inspector Nair initiated the plan, sir, but I agreed. It was a joint decision." He glanced at Nair. "We take joint responsibility."

The DCC nodded. "A problem shared is a problem halved, eh? Well, you've given Cochin Police a great deal to do on a very wet evening. And the Vice Squad. But I suppose there's never a good time to bust a high-end brothel operating out of a prestigious city centre location." The DCC fixed them with a glare. "I should reprimand you both and send you packing back to Mattancherry. You've jeopardised this operation. For what purpose, exactly?"

Nair sat up. "We had no other choice, sir. It was a human trafficking situation. Sex slavery. Completely unacceptable. We had to act."

The DCC stared at him. "Your brief was to watch and report, not intervene. Couldn't you have done that? And reported it later?"

Koshy spoke up again. "But if we hadn't gone in, sir, we wouldn't have known. These criminals would just have carried on with their filthy business. And we would have been none the wiser."

The DCC nodded at Koshy. "So you're standing with your colleague, Koshy? You'll take the fall as well? Very noble, but it might be an impediment to your progress in the police. Sub-Inspector Nair's card is already marked. Never has a probationary Sub-Inspector generated so much ire in Cochin Police. Sure you want to join him?"

Koshy said nothing. Nair made to speak, but the DCC raised a hand.

"Anyway, the IG is pleased. That counts for something. And I can't say the result is entirely to our disadvantage. Two of the 'Relaxation Lounge' customers were prominent local politicians. One of them has been a thorn in our side. No longer. We have some leverage. Which we will use." The DCC turned to his counterpart. "Vijay, fill the Sub-Inspectors in. I have to speak to the Vice Squad. Don't get up." The DCC rose to his feet and turned for the door.

"Sir!" Nair said. The DCC stopped. "Sorry, sir, but the women? The sex workers? What will happen to them?"

The DCC studied Nair. "You needn't worry, Nair. Vice Squad has placed the eight girls you liberated in secure accommodation, in the care of a charitable organisation for trafficked women. There are constables posted outside. Tomorrow, Vice will gather their stories and prepare the prosecution. In time, the girls will be returned to their families, if that is their wish, or they will be taught some other means of making a living. Satisfied?"

Nair nodded. "Yes, sir. Thank you."

The DCC nodded back. "That is the one thing that has saved you both. I'll be back in an hour. By then, you'd better have a plan to get us back on track. I'm sure you'll manage it. Don't disappoint me a second time."

Vijay flipped open a folder. The Customs Officer was lean and clean shaven with short, curly hair and a beaky nose. He glanced up and saw that he had their full attention.

"Mr. Bin Jamal." Vijay said. "An interesting individual. UAE national. Widely travelled. Several visits to the US and UK, Azerbaijan, Italy, Hong Kong, Malacca, Egypt, Australia and South Korea. No prior entry stamps for India. He claims he's a businessman involved in 'venture capital' and that this visit is a business trip. Not very forthcoming about who his business partners are. Just said he's 'exploring opportunities'. Booked in for a stay at the Grand Vembanad for a week." Vijay glanced up at them again. "We have a team searching the hotel room. He insists on a lawyer and refuses to say more until he has one."

"Has he been arrested?" Nair asked. "Formally?"

"No," Vijay said. "Did you arrest him? Formally? When you found him?"

Nair shook his head. "No. We only have 24 hours from arrest—"

"Before he has to be presented to a magistrate," Koshy said. "That's not a lot of time."

"Exactly." Vijay said. "Which is why we're holding him in preventative detention as a hostile alien. We'll have to make progress quickly before the lawyers get involved. Or release him without charge."

"Can't we prosecute him for engaging in prostitution?" Nair said.

Vijay shook his head. "Not unless he was involved in the business of running the brothel, no. There's no provision in the Indian Penal Code to charge a customer. Bin Jamal claims he thought he was having a massage, that the two girls tied him up and began beating him. To extort money from him." Vijay smirked. "He says he's the victim and the women, the offenders. He's insisting we prosecute them."

Nair snorted. "Both girls were barely five feet tall. And

underfed. I find it difficult to believe that they could have hogtied him."

Vijay nodded. "Quite. It doesn't wash. Vice Squad will cross-check his testimony with what the girls say. Regardless, even if the girls confirm they were doing as he instructed, we won't have a legal basis to prosecute. Paying someone to tie you up and beat you is not a crime."

"Anything on his phone?" Koshy said.

"That's more promising," Vijay replied. "There's a meeting taking place. Tomorrow evening. At Very Famous Spice House. Bin Jamal is meeting Peter John. John is the proprietor of that establishment. And our prime suspect in the smuggling operation. That may be an opportunity. If we can get Bin Jamal to co-operate. We could wire him up. The problem is, we don't have any means of forcing Jamal to co-operate. And I don't think appealing to his sense of justice will work."

Nair glanced at Koshy. Koshy nodded and reached into his pocket.

"We may have a way," Nair said. "Koshy?"

Koshy slid the phone across the table to Vijay. Vijay picked it up. His face crumpled with curiosity, then split into a wide grin.

"Oh, yes." Vijay chuckled. "Oh, yes. I think that will do very nicely indeed."

25

Peter John was in his upstairs office when the SUV pulled up on the street below. John's office was at the rear of Very Famous Spice House and looked out onto the canal. John had been studying the ships berthed on the opposite side of the channel through his binoculars. The lights in the office were off and, as dusk fell, John was certain that he could not be seen. John was a careful man—it was attention to detail that had got him this far. He paid heed to what went on around him.

The container ship and the oil tanker had been berthed at Mattancherry Wharf for a week. Today, a new vessel had slid in between the other two: an Indian naval ship, pennant number T99. He'd looked it up: *INS Chawara*, a Car Nicobar-class fast-attack craft designed for coastal patrol and surveillance. His binoculars played over the deck, noting nothing unusual about the activity onboard. He had watched many ships dock and knew the rituals well. Smaller naval vessels often berthed at Mattancherry Wharf if the wharves at the Naval Base on the other side of Willingdon Island were full.

John heard the car's engine, lowered his binoculars, and peered out through the window. He sighed with relief. The Audi was one of Moopan's vehicles—he recognised the number plate. Relief was replaced by dismay as the passenger door opened and the Arab stepped out. The Arab was wearing a full Arab costume. This was supposed to be a discreet meeting—the Arab should have known better. Still, John knew from long experience that there was an inverse relationship between wealth and sense. Bin Jamal was very wealthy. And clearly idiotic.

John was about to call down to his men when he heard the gates swing open. The Arab waved the vehicle on. The engine note rose, and the Audi disappeared from view into the loading bay. Bin Jamal tarried. He swivelled in place, taking in the expanse of the Kollam-Kottapuram Waterway.

John resisted the urge to shout through the window bars. Instead, he muttered under his breath.

"Get inside, you idiot! Get in!"

A party of Caucasian tourists trooped past from where the Bolghatty ferry had docked a few minutes earlier. An Indian tour guide led the party, clipboard under his arm. The foreigners were clearly Americans. John could tell from their excessively loud chatter. Americans were always loud. Like Australians. They seemed to think the world was interested in anything they had to say. He supposed that too came with wealth.

The tourists' destination was the Coconut Tree restaurant a few doors down—it was a regular pilgrimage for tour groups organised by the Grand Vembanad Hotel. The chatter turned to gasps and exclamations as the group split around the Arab standing in their path. John's dismay turned to disbelief as a pair of tourists approached the Arab and said something to him. One of them held out a phone.

Bin Jamal nodded. John's jaw fell open as they bunched together for a selfie, the Arab putting his arms around the two obese women on either side. The Arab said something to them and the women cackled like crows. The Arab waved them goodbye before turning and sauntering in to the loading bay.

John picked up his binoculars and scanned the opposite shore. Nothing. No one on the naval ship appeared to have noticed, nor indeed had anyone else. Cursing, he pulled the window shutters closed and ran down the stairs.

The Arab was standing in front of the Audi, both hands on his hips. Next to him stood a plump man in a white uniform, who John presumed was the driver. The driver's face was unfamiliar, but Moopan had many in his operation. John assumed the man was trustworthy. Moopan wouldn't have sent him along if he wasn't. Two of John's men waited on the visitors, Raghu the foreman and Jibby, who worked in the warehouse. Another of John's employees was on watch duty at the front.

John had been concerned when he hadn't heard from the Arab. Moopan's driver was supposed to have called him after the Arab arrived, but there had been nothing. Moopan had sent Raghu to the Grand Vembanad Hotel. Raghu had bribed a concierge. Yes, the Arab had arrived. He had checked in, then left shortly after. He hadn't returned that evening or the next day. It looked like the Arab had disappeared.

John had sent Bin Jamal the briefest of texts, confirming the time and date of the meeting, but had received no reply. His anxiety had risen. He'd tried to contact Moopan, but his calls had gone unanswered. John had despatched another fellow to Kacheripady; he had returned to report that

Amber Villa was deserted. The gates were locked and the gate guard absent. That had troubled John further. But now, the Arab was here. It was time to get on with things and conclude what needed to be concluded.

The Arab's glance fell on John as he clambered down the steps.

"Ah," the Arab said. "Finally. The boss man is arrive. Very good. Very good. Now we can start business, yes? *Salaam alaikum. Kaif al halak?*[1]"

John smiled and put out a hand. "Welcome. Welcome, Mr. Bin Jamal. I am Peter John. We have communicated—"

"*Aiwa*[2], *aiwa.*" The Arab was taller than John had expected, nearly six feet, and with a rather proud nose. The man was sunburnt, so dark he could have passed for a native, except for the ridiculously bushy beard. John knew Bedouin spent a lot of time in the desert with their camels, which explained the man's complexion.

The Arab ignored John's hand. "No shake hand. *Haram*[3], you understand? We say hello in Indian style." The Arab put his palms together in a namaste. "This is correct, yes?"

John mirrored the gesture. "Yes. Yes," he said eagerly. "That is correct. Welcome to Cochin. Did you have a pleasant trip?"

The Arab cocked his head. "Listen, *ya habibi*[4], you are nice man. I like you. Small. Brown. But Abdullah Bin Jamal is busy, busy man also. Let us go business, *insha'Allah*[5]. *Yallah*[6]. *Yallah.*" The Arab waved both hands, urging everyone on. "*Yallah!* Let us go! Where is cargo? You show me! Now."

John nodded at Raghu, the foreman. "Show him," he said in Malayalam.

Raghu turned and headed into the warehouse. The Arab

and the driver followed. John grabbed the driver by the arm. "Not you," he said. "You stay here. You don't need to see this. What's your name? I haven't seen you before."

The driver blinked at him. "No, sir. I am new. My name is Madhavan. Mr. Moopan said—"

"Where is Moopan?" John said, cutting him off. "I've been trying to reach him."

The driver glanced around. "Left the country, sir. In a hurry. Some problem with one of the other drivers. Driver Chacko. Disappeared. With a consignment." The driver leaned in and lowered his voice. "Police may be involved. So the boss thought it best to leave the country till things cool down. Best not to contact him, sir. He will contact you."

John cursed. "Bloody hell! And he couldn't inform me! Idiot! And you! You were meant to ring me when the Arab arrived. Why didn't you?"

The driver shook his head. "Instructions, sir. Mr. Moopan said to keep all communications to a minimum. He also said I was to accompany the Arabic fellow wherever—"

"No." John glanced over at Jibby. "Jibby will keep you company. You stay here."

"Mad!" The Arab was at the inner door to the warehouse. "Mad! Come here, *ya habibi*! Why you hide there? Come!"

John walked over to the Arab. "He's staying here, Mr. Bin Jamal. Safer that way."

The Arab looked perturbed. "But—"

John gestured inwards. "Please. He will still be there when we are finished."

The Arab looked like he was about to argue. His upper lip curled. His eyes glared. He muttered under his breath. He sounded like he was cursing. "*Min fadlak! Shukran!*[7] *Min fadlak!*"

“Please,” John said. His tone was firm. “After you.”

With a huff, Sub-Inspector Vasanth Nair turned his back on John and, with some trepidation, stepped through the door.

26

The warehouse was immense, much larger than the narrow frontage of the premises suggested. They had dismantled the dividing walls between Famous Spice House and its neighbours. It was a labyrinth, formed of piles of pallets, crates, cartons and sacks, heaped above head height. There was barely enough space between for two men to walk abreast. A blue-grey pall came from fluorescent tubes set vertically into steel uprights, throwing their path in partial shadow. Overhead, glimmers of light played off aluminium roofing. The heady smell of spice saturated the air, so thick it made Nair's nose run.

After three turns, Nair had lost his bearings completely. He hoped that the radio strapped around his waist was still transmitting from the microphone concealed beneath his clothing. Nair thought he had done a good job impersonating Bin Jamal. Bin Jamal had refused to co-operate, despite the threats of the compromising photographs making their way out into the wider world.

"I know it is you!" Bin Jamal had almost spat at them. "If this photograph is release, I know it is you! And my lawyer will sue you! Yes! Sue you! I have many, many friends! In your government. You understand? I will see you fire!"

They had had no alternative plan. Koshy zoomed off to a second-hand bookshop and returned with an English-Arabic dictionary for pilgrims travelling to Mecca. Nair had tried to commit some of it to memory, but he had had little time. Nair figured it was the manner in which things were said that mattered. People saw what they expected to see. Peter John would expect an Arab, and an Arab would be what he saw. Nair had been confident it would work, despite Koshy's misgivings. So far, it seemed to be working.

They came to a stop in front of a stack of sacks indistinguishable from any other. A knife appeared in Raghu's hands. Nair was instantly on edge. Raghu bent forward and slit a sack open. He reached in, then turned around, holding out his open palm. In it lay shrivelled grey-green leaves.

Nair didn't need to bend forward or sniff. The smell was overpowering at two feet of separation.

"Cannabis," John said from behind. "Best quality. From Idukki, high in the hills. It's our very own strain. We've tested it. 33% THC content. One of the strongest in the world. You don't need very much. Which means more profit per gram. For you. And for me."

Nair shook his head in mock admiration. "*Ya habibi! Ya habibi!* This makes Abdullah very happy man. Good! Very good!"

John looked pleased. "Glad to hear. We have two tonnes ready to ship out. Once we receive the payment. When will that be?"

Nair pretended to think. "I will check. With my company. I call them tonight. How you would like payment?"

John looked puzzled. "The usual way."

Nair nodded. "Ah. Yes. The usual way." He racked his brain. "Yes. The usual way. *Min fadlak.*"

"You do know what the usual way is?" John said. His brows furrowed. He peered at Nair. "Don't you? I thought you dealt with finance."

Nair waved at him. "I deal with top-level finance, *ya habibi.* Dollars. Cryptocurrency. Millions. Billions. My associates deal with small transactions." Nair paused. "So, how do you like to be paid? I will arrange."

"Gold." John said. "Bullion. Sovereigns. Anything that is portable and tradeable. That is how we are usually paid."

Nair nodded. "Of course. No problem. No problem. And what about the *khat*?"

"*Khat?*" John thought a moment. "Of course. You want to see the *khat* as well? It's just this way. After you."

Nair nodded and took two steps before he felt a strong arm wrap around his chest. And something wickedly sharp at his throat.

Raghu had closed behind him. The edge of Raghu's blade rested against Nair's Adam's apple.

John stepped in front of Nair, his eyes cold.

"How do you know about the *kha*t?" John said, his voice low. "We've never sold you any. That's a completely different operation." John stepped in close. "Who are you? You're not Abdullah Bin Jamal. Who are you?"

John grabbed Nair's beard. And pulled. It came away in his hands.

"It's time for tea!" Nair shouted at the top of his voice. "It's time for tea!"

That's all he managed before Raghu kicked his knees out from behind him and he crumpled to the floor. Nair spat dust out of his mouth and pushed himself to sitting.

The blade of the knife was three inches away from his face.

"Who are you?" John said, leaning down. "Who the hell are you? Speak, or I'll cut your tongue out."

Nair wiped the dust off his lips. "Sub-Inspector Vasanth Nair. Mattancherry Police. And you, idiot, are under arrest."

Raghu glanced at his boss. John took a step back. Nair continued.

"Put the knife down, idiot. And surrender. Any second now, your door is going to be broken in. And this place will swarm with police. There's no escape."

A blow between his shoulder blades sent Nair sprawling onto his front. He grunted as Raghu kneeled on him. The man's weight crushed the air out of him. Nair felt Raghu's hand scrabbling at his clothing. He felt the tip of the blade in the middle of his back, then a sharp pain running down his spine.

"Ow!" Nair screamed. He wriggled but could not move. "You bastard!"

Cool air caressed Nair's skin. Raghu had split Nair's robe open at the back. Raghu's rough fingers tugged at the waistband of Nair's underwear.

"There's a wire!" Raghu shouted to John. "He's wearing a bug!"

The bulging of John's eyes was the last thing Nair saw of him before John raced into the shadows.

Raghu leaned forward. His breath hissed in Nair's ear.

"I hate the police!" Raghu hissed. The point of the blade danced in front of Nair's eyes. "I bloody hate them!"

"Come on now, Raghu." Nair's voice was measured. "Don't do this. You can't get away. Give it up. You're surrounded—"

Raghu grunted. "I don't hear anything. Sure your radio

is working, Sub-Inspector Idiot? I don't think so. These walls are thick. Which means it's just you and me. Which eye is it to be first? Left or right? You choose."

Nair went still. "Is there an alternative option?" he asked in a small voice.

And then the earth shook.

It was the opportunity Nair had been waiting for. As Raghu stabbed in, Nair grabbed the wrist with his hands and twisted it. Nair flicked his head away—the blade went wide, just missing his left earlobe. Nair kicked out with one foot, found the earth, twisted his hips. He felt Raghu's weight shift. Nair pulled Raghu's wrist in and heaved himself over.

Raghu crashed down on his side. Nair followed him round. They were face to face on their sides in a churning cloud of dust. Raghu's feet scrabbled for purchase. The knife zigged and zagged between them, darting towards Raghu, then back at Nair as the centre of their mortal struggle shifted one way, then the other.

Raghu's teeth were gritted. His eyes glimmered with rage. Raghu's breath burst over Nair's face in grunts.

Raghu kicked at Nair, the Sub-Inspector deflecting the strike with his thigh. The pain was a dull burst, like a misfiring firework. Nair kicked back, connecting with Raghu's kneecap. Raghu howled, and for a moment, Nair had the advantage. He wrenched Raghu's wrists, using the leverage of Raghu's locked elbows to put strain on the man's joints. The knife slipped out of Raghu's grasp. Nair swatted it away but, in doing so, had to release his grip. Raghu was quick to retaliate.

Callused hands clamped around Nair's throat. Nair batted at them, but to no avail. Raghu clambered up and leaned over Nair. A gob of spittle spattered on Nair's cheek. A knee crashed into Nair's stomach, winding him.

Nair's vision flickered. In the distance, he could hear his mother's voice. Calling.

Nair kicked at the earth with his heels, but it was useless. He was like a fish spitted on a spike.

His vision blurred. His mother's voice grew fainter, replaced by another sound. This was a low rumbling, born of a beast's throat. It grew louder and louder, a growl, a roar, a bellow.

Nair could see it now, in the blackness of his vision. A huge water buffalo padded towards him, saliva hanging in ropes from its snout, great horns forking the air. And on its back, seated cross-legged, sat Yama, the God of Death. Yama grinned at him and raised his right hand. In it dangled a noose, the noose the God looped around the necks of the dead as he dragged them away to Purgatory.

"Is it time, Lord?" Nair heard himself ask. "Is it my time? I have things to do—"

Yama shook his head and lowered the noose. "Not yet. Do what you must, mortal. But quickly. Someday, I will return. For you."

And then the vision disappeared.

Suddenly, Nair could breathe again. He took great, hacking breaths, his lungs filling with the spice-tainted air. His vision strobed, then flashed, then returned, grey-scale first, then colour, tinted red.

Someone was screaming. It was high-pitched and wordless, yelps, squeals, pleas. Someone else was growling. Nair propped himself up on one elbow.

Raghu was rolling across the floor. It was Raghu that was howling. Raghu's heels kicked air. Raghu's right hand flailed in the dust. His eyes were wide with dread, fixed on the large German Shepherd that had his left forearm between his jaws. Rex growled and bit down as blood spattered across the floor. Nair heard the crunching of teeth on bone.

Lord Yama had departed. And Rex had arrived.

27

Nair found his way back by heading for the noise. Halfway through the maze, he bashed into Koshy, running the other way. Koshy came up short, grabbing Nair's shoulders to stop himself.

"Nair!" Koshy's face was pale. "Thank God! I thought you were a goner! Are you alright? Let me look at you."

"I'm fine. Dusty but intact." Nair replied, but Koshy would brook no argument. He spun Nair this way and that.

Koshy gasped. "Bloody hell! You're cut! There's blood on your back. And on this blasted nightdress. Come on! Quickly! Into the light." Koshy grabbed Nair by the shoulders and propelled him back through the door.

The loading bay was teeming with people: Cochin Police in khaki, Customs officers in white, and a platoon of soldiers in berets and fatigues. Two men lay spread-eagled on the floor, guarded by two more police dogs and their handlers.

The rear gates hung off their hinges, staved in by a lorry driven in at speed. The lorry had shunted the Audi forward; the SUV lay crumpled, its nose wrapped around a pillar.

There was a strong smell of petrol. Three firemen moved carefully over the floor, sprinkling absorbent from buckets onto the spill.

"Hey you!" Koshy shouted at a constable. "Get the ambulance! The Sub-Inspector is injured! Quickly, you idiot! Run!"

Nair tried to speak, but Koshy spun him round again. Nair felt Koshy prod him.

"Thank God!" Koshy said. "It's shallow. And it's stopped oozing. You'll have a nice scar, Nair, but I think you'll survive." Nair turned around. "Stupid bloody idea, Nair! Another one of yours! We should never have done it."

Nair waved him away. "Oh, relax. Mission accomplished, right?" A thought struck him. "John! Peter John! Where is he?"

Koshy grinned. "Oh, him. He got away." He watched Nair scowl. "From us. But not away. Come look!"

Nair held the split ends of the robe together with one hand behind his back. Koshy led him out the rear entrance, shoving policemen aside.

They were on the road, looking out onto the waterway. There were barriers erected on the footpath on either side, behind which a throng of heads bobbed and jigged for a better view. Koshy pointed to the right.

"Look! There he comes!"

Nair peered out. It was difficult to see, but he could just make out, in the middle of the watercourse, the trail of a silver wake heading towards them.

"He got in a boat," Koshy said. "Headed south, but now he's discovered that there's a Customs cutter at that end of the channel. So he's doubled back."

The thud-thud-thud of a diesel engine reverberated across the water.

"Well, why the hell are we standing here?" Nair said. "Let's get after him! There must be a boat somewhere—"

Koshy laid a hand on Nair's shoulder. His grip was firm. "No, no, no. You're a casualty. You're not going anywhere. Just wait. The Navy's on to him."

As if on cue, a blinding glare flashed out across the water at them. Nair saw arms rise to cover eyes, heads turn away, before the glare dipped towards the water. An instant later, it found the boat.

John was in the stern of a shallow-hulled skiff, right hand on the outboard motor. John flinched at the light, the steering hand jerking away and sending the vessel's bow veering towards the near shore before he corrected. John tucked his head in and hunched down. The pitch of the engine note climbed as the craft picked up speed and the bow rose out of the water. John was making a run for it.

"ATTENTION! THIS IS THE NAVY! STOP YOUR ENGINE!"

The words were deafening and metallic. They came from the Fast Attack Craft berthed across the water.

John shook his head and tried to make himself smaller. The skiff was abreast of them now, surging towards the head of the channel, from where John could crest the point of Willingdon Island and head out to sea.

"FINAL WARNING!" sounded. To no avail.

Nair thought someone had let off fireworks. It was a series of bangs, but so fast that they almost merged into one. A stream of fire arced out from the ship, streaming down towards the water's surface.

The onlookers screamed and flinched. The bow of John's boat disintegrated, the wood splintering into fragments that spun up and out of the spotlight's beam. With half its hull destroyed, the skiff's momentum drove it into the water until the engine submerged and died.

A roar of approval went up from the crowd, followed by applause and whistles. The spotlight played across the water. There, bobbing up and down, was Peter John, looking for all the world like a drowned rat.

"Mission accomplished," Nair said, grinning. "At last."

"Indeed." Koshy put an arm around his shoulders. "Hang on to your robe, Nair. Your rear end is hanging out. Let's get you changed into some proper gear, get those wounds tended to. And then it really will be time for tea."

28

It was almost five months later that Sub-Inspector Koshy had occasion to call on Sub-Inspector Nair again. Nair was in his office on the second floor of Customs House, processing paper, when he heard a knock at the open door.

"Koshy!" Nair rose to his feet. "Bloody hell, man. You're looking well."

Koshy was. He'd lost ten kilos, he told Nair. And he was getting married. "Which is why I came," Koshy said. He laid a gold envelope on the desk. "Here's your invitation. It would be an honour if you would come."

Nair blinked. He picked up the envelope, examined it, then laid it down on the desk. "It would be my pleasure. Thank you. And congratulations! Who's the unhappy girl?"

Koshy grinned and scratched his chest. "Her name's Tina. She's an architect. From Trivandrum. My family and her family have some friends in common. Introductions were made, and we hit it off."

Nair clapped Koshy on the shoulder. "I never thought

you'd settle down, Koshy. You're cutting down on the drinking, I hope. And all the rest?"

Koshy looked furtive. "Well, not quite. No. I'm not married yet. But I've promised I will. Tina pointed out that it doesn't do for a Sub-Inspector of the Vice Squad to, well, have vices. Anyway, how are you? How is Customs and Excise suiting you? Not quite Mattancherry, is it?"

Nair shook his head. "That it is not. And thank God. I have you to thank for arranging it."

Koshy waved Nair's thanks away. "Least I could do. At last count, I owed you two. And the Deputy Commissioner was receptive to the idea that you take my place."

"We're even." Nair said. "All debts are repaid, so far as I'm concerned. I'm surprised you opted for the Vice Squad, though. I didn't see that coming."

"Neither did I. It was that episode at Smiley Silks that got me thinking. There's an entire subculture of evil in operation here, Nair. I want to be part of taking it down."

Nair shook his head. "I never thought I'd have heard that from you. You said nothing like that back in Mattancherry."

Koshy shrugged. "Times change, and we must change with them. Speaking of which, I heard Kurien's retired early."

"Oh? I hadn't heard."

Koshy had a knowing look. "Forced to. He's under investigation. Along with a few others. The new government is taking a hard line on corruption. There are quite a few large trees falling in the forest, leaving space for young saplings. Like us. And what about you, Nair? No plans of marriage? Still living the ascetic yogic lifestyle? And what about fish? Still a vegetable? Or—" Koshy paused at the look on Nair's face. Nair's gaze was elsewhere. "What is it?"

Nair was staring at the TV on the wall. It was on the rolling news channel, but the sound was off.

Koshy blinked at what he was seeing. "Turn the sound on, Nair."

Nair scrabbled for the remote control. They watched it unfold live. The commentary was breathless.

"We're broadcasting live from Cubbon Park, just across the road from the Vidhana Soudha. Today is the State Opening of Parliament, which appears to be under some kind of terrorist attack. Just minutes earlier, a flying object crashed into the main entrance. No explosions or damage to the building, but we've seen fallen bodies on the steps. Just now, a cadre of armed troops raced out of the main entrance. They've surrounded the building. There are sirens everywhere and lots of police activity. We saw ambulances and fire engines race through the gates.

As you can see, the firemen have deployed their hoses. We can't see a fire, or smoke, but they're directing the spray at the verandahs of the ground floor. And look! There's movement! Yes, there are more armed men running down the stairs now, from inside the building. And there's a police officer there with them. He's carrying something. Let's see if we can zoom in."

THEY WATCHED the grainy picture in extreme close-up. A figure bent over the railing, khaki police uniform sodden with the play of the firehoses. The man had something in his arms, a small bundle. A child. He bent over and handed the child off to a fireman waiting below. The child's body was limp. The fireman raced away. The policeman straightened up, and for one moment, looked out, directly into the camera. There was a flash of dark fury beneath thunderous brows before he looked away. And turned away.

Later, that image would feature on the front pages of every national and international newspaper. The image that symbolised a new war in a new age: agro-terrorists attacking an institution of government using bio-engineered pesticides. The image that captured Inspector Chatpati, reluctant hero of the Vidhana Soudha Incident, at what was simultaneously his finest professional hour and his lowest personal point.

It was at that moment that Sub-Inspector Nair knew his future lay elsewhere. Lord Yama's words resounded in his ears.

"Do what you must, mortal. But quickly. Someday, I will return. For you."

"I'm leaving," Nair said, his eyes on the screen. "It's time to move on. Life is short. And I have a lot to do."

"What?" Koshy said, staring at Nair. "What do you mean you're leaving? You barely got here. Where are you going?"

Nair nodded at the screen. "Where is that happening?"

"Bangalore. In Karnataka. It's Bangalore."

"That's where," Nair said. "There."

NOTES

CHAPTER 1

1. Grandmother (Malayalam)
2. Palace (Malayalam)
3. A now-defunct kingdom that, at its peak, covered most of south Kerala.
4. A loose long-sleeved collarless shirt (kurta) worn over loose trousers (pyjama)

CHAPTER 2

1. Bananas fried in batter. A teatime snack. Hugely calorific. (Malayalam)
2. Literally 'story play'. A form of classical dance unique to Kerala. (Malayalam)
3. A warrior prince in the Indian epic, the Mahabharata.
4. Hand gestures which, along with eye movement, facial expression and body position, are used by Kathakali dancers to convey meaning.
5. Another South Indian dance form.

CHAPTER 3

1. Member of the State Parliament.
2. A 500cc motorcycle, the longest running motorcycle in continuous production.
3. A steamed pancake made out of fermented rice batter and coconut milk. A popular breakfast dish.
4. A native of the north-eastern Indian state of Assam, a region renowned for the quality of its tea.

CHAPTER 5

1. Secondary School Leaving Certificate. Equivalent to a high school diploma.
2. Illegally obtained or undeclared income.

CHAPTER 9

1. A sarong, for all practical purposes.
2. A roadside eatery serving cheap street food.
3. A Hindu deity popular in South India. Embodies truth and justice.
4. A steamed cake made of rice flour.
5. Layered flatbreads.
6. Black chickpeas.

CHAPTER 10

1. An annual harvest festival widely celebrated in Kerala. Onam commemorates the good rule of the mythical king Mahabali who is thought to return to visit his people on this day.

CHAPTER 11

1. A roadside restaurant or truck-stop
2. A savoury fried snack made of lentils.
3. An armed militant group espousing radical communism.

CHAPTER 12

1. Short for First Information Received, the report created by the police when they receive information about a suspected crime.
2. A loose flannel vest, worn as an undergarment.

CHAPTER 15

1. The state of transcendental enlightenment achieved by release from the cycle of death and rebirth.

NOTES

CHAPTER 17

1. Aka Lord Ganesha, an elephant-headed Hindu God. Patron of arts, the God of Beginnings and the Remover of Obstacles. Rides a rat.

CHAPTER 18

1. A shoulder-length headdress
2. Black cord placed on top of the head to keep the *ghutra* in place
3. Ankle-length, long-sleeved robe.
4. An annual temple festival held in Trishur. Features richly caparisoned elephants, grand umbrellas and fireworks.

CHAPTER 19

1. Traditional Indian washerman

CHAPTER 21

1. Literally 'rubbed by being stomped on'. (Malayalam) In this context, a traditional massage technique in which the client is lathered in oil and lies on the floor while the masseur uses bare feet.
2. A celestial nymph
3. A long skirt, typically embroidered and adorned with mirror work.

CHAPTER 22

1. A female demon.

CHAPTER 23

1. A form of martial arts unique to Kerala. Proponents are versed in unarmed combat as well as the use of weapons such as sword and staff.

CHAPTER 24

1. A long bamboo stick, excellent for cracking skulls.

CHAPTER 25

1. "Peace be with you. How are you?" (Arabic)
2. "Yes" or "Of course" (Arabic)
3. Forbidden by Islamic law.
4. "Darling." (Arabic)
5. "God willing." (Arabic)
6. "Let's go!" or "Hurry up!" (Arabic)
7. "Please! Thank you! Please!" (Arabic)

THE TENDER COCONUT TAMASHA

1. The building that houses the State Parliament
2. "Well done!" (Hindi)
3. A tuk-tuk by another name.
4. The term used to refer to the century of colonial British rule, ending with Indian independence in 1947.
5. Translates as 'oppressed'. Term used by people belonging to the lowest Hindu castes to refer to themselves.
6. The Hoysala is Traffic Division's standard patrol vehicle. Named for the imperial dynasty that had ruled Bangalore six centuries ago, it is far from majestic, being a hulking SUV-type thing with three red lights, two different klaxon tones and a roof-mounted loudspeaker to harangue road users with.
7. The official language of the state of Karnataka, of which Bangalore is the capital.
8. A neighbouring state.
9. A traditional form of theatre, often based on Hindu epics, involving face-paint, costumes, drums, declamation and grand conflict. Typically performed in the open air. Performances last all night.

AUTHOR'S NOTE

Reviews are the life blood of the independent author's career.

I'd be grateful if you would consider leaving an honest review wherever you bought this book. I read, and value, every one.

If you received this book as a free copy, please add the following line (or similar) to your review, otherwise certain platforms get annoyed.

"I received a free copy of this book and am voluntarily leaving a review."

LEAVE A REVIEW

ACKNOWLEDGMENTS

My first book, The Tender Coconut Tamasha, was proof of concept. Was there really a market for a modern Indian cosy mystery? Does anyone want to read about murder by coconut?

It's the overwhelmingly positive response of readers that's encouraged me to carry on writing and it is to them that my thanks must go first. Rob Arthur was one of the first to feed back about how much he enjoyed the book. Rob knows Bangalore well, and it was heartening to hear I'd hit the right geographical notes.

"The J-Team" is my crack support unit. Nothing makes the final cut without them. Undying gratitude to Kalpana and Tanya.

Special thanks to Francis Colaso, IPS (retired), former Director General of Police of Karnataka, for his kind observations about policing in the real world, thankfully mostly full of honest people, quite distinct from fiction.

My gratitude goes to Bob McDevitt, author Gordon Brown and the team behind Scotland's premier crime writing festival, Bloody Scotland, who gave me the opportunity to pitch the book at the 2022 festival in Stirling and do my first ever book signing. If you're a fan of crime fiction, I would strongly recommend visiting the festival, usually in September every year. It's criminally good.

I couldn't end without mentioning Anthony Horowitz,

a modern-day literary giant, who I was privileged to spend some time with at Bloody Scotland. It was an unforgettable experience.

About the Author

Joe Chacko lives in Scotland.

He works as an anaesthetist at a rather large, rather ugly hospital. When not putting people to sleep, he can be found planting things the wrong way up in his allotment and playing bass guitar not very well.

He's currently working on the next instalment in the Inspector Chatpati mysteries.

Find out more at www.joechacko.co.uk.

If you enjoyed this book, please leave an honest review wherever you bought it.

twitter.com/joechackoauthor

instagram.com/joechackoauthor

goodreads.com/joechackoauthor

amazon.com/Joe-Chacko/e/B08SHLB4HS

ALSO BY JOE CHACKO

BANGALORE CIVIL NUISANCE UNIT SERIES

THE TENDER COCONUT TAMASHA

Book 1

A Page Turner Award Finalist! Available on all major platforms.

Join Inspector Hari Chatpati and the Bangalore Civil Nuisance Unit as they try to solve the mystery of a series of inexplicable deaths linked (inexplicably) to coconuts.

THE DISAPPEARING DHOBI

Book 2

Release date: early-2023

The CNU investigates the theft of dirty laundry. Why has the *dhobi* disappeared? And why do the residents of Regal Inheritance Apartments deny all knowledge of the *dhobi's* existence? It's a grand conspiracy of the unexpected.

THE ARMS OF DURGA

Book 3

Release date: mid-2023

Inspector Chatpati faces his greatest challenge as a series of gruesome ritual murders plague Bangalore. Is it the work of human hands? Or has the Hindu warrior goddess Durga really returned to the world to deal justice on the wicked?

THE TENDER COCONUT TAMASHA

AN EXTRACT FROM THE NEXT IN THE SERIES.

THE TENDER COCONUT TAMASHA

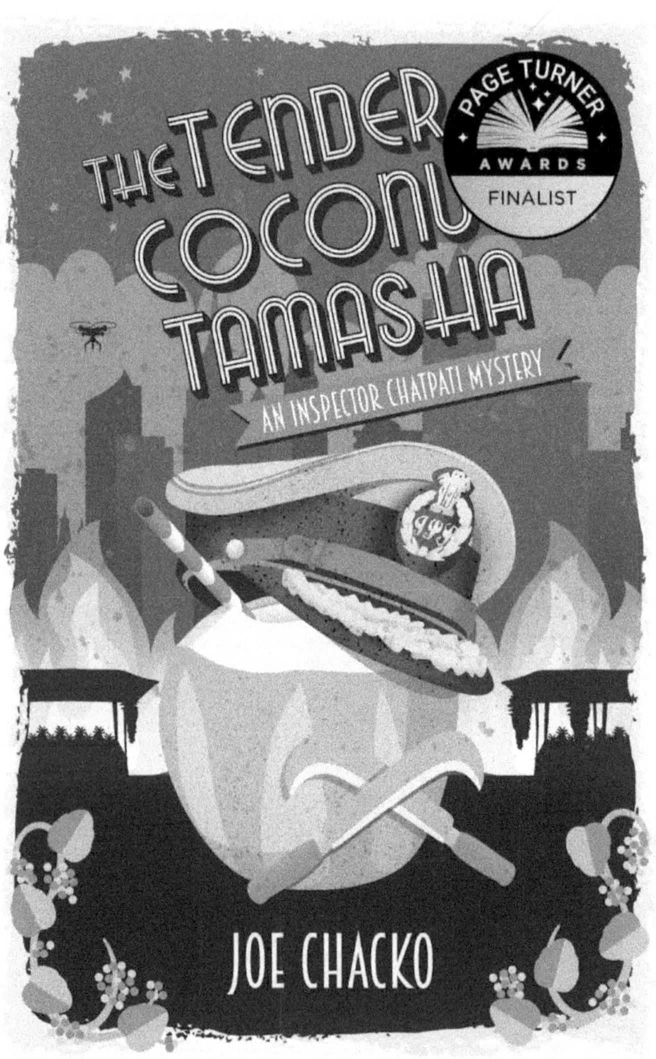

CHAPTER 1: Date of Expiry

Mohan Rao hadn't expected his Tuesday morning to end the way it did. It had begun, like all his weekdays, with a run in Cubbon Park.

It was the best part of the day, the first rays of sunlight glinting off the steely glass facades of the office blocks and hotels that ensnared the city's ancient, woody heart. The avenues were cool under leaf, the obstacles a mere handful of perambulating pensioners, no real impediment to the sure-footed.

One such non-impediment, Colonel Rajvir Singh, Indian Army (retired), memory still bayonet keen, would recognise Mohan Rao from the photograph in the next day's Bangalore Herald and remark on it to his wife, who said nothing.

K. Senthil, street vendor, at his usual spot opposite the Maharajah's statue, would describe how Rao had stopped by at his usual time, paid for his usual refreshment and downed it in the usual single gulp.

The doorman at ParkVue Apartments would report that Rao had staggered, rather than walked, into the lobby.

The lift attendant would say, when asked, that Rao had looked sweaty and pale.

Dr. Anand Acharya, general practitioner, would confirm that Rao had rung for an urgent appointment at 8.13am. "Feeling unwell" read the receptionist's note. "Abdominal pain. Nausea."

An ambulance had been despatched, as per the corporate insurance policy, but the ambulance crew received no answer at Rao's door.

The apartment manager, duly summoned, had found Rao in the kitchen, face down in a pool of frothy vomit.

Had he been given the opportunity to reflect, Mohan Rao might have declared himself satisfied with the weave of his life so far. The private education his parents couldn't really afford had led to a fine job with a good salary. He had left the small town of his birth for a high-rise in the big city.

His entry into adult life had been ballistic, his arc on the ascendant.

Weightless, Rao felt not the clutch of casual circumstance that flattens many such trajectories.

Death grounds every mortal expectation.

This is what Inspector Hari Chatpati would discover some days later, thanks to the angry Austrian tourist and the travel agent who was anything but.

Chapter 2: No Hero's Welcome

At around the time Mohan Rao died, Inspector Chatpati was dying his own kind of death. There were many things that annoyed Chatpati but none more than a meeting with the Assistant Commissioner of Police.

The Headquarters of Central Division on Kasturba Road had been a drab, soot-stained villa, built during the British Raj, until the addition of a steel carbuncle five storeys tall. The ACP's office was on the top floor and commanded a fine view of the city. Had Chatpati looked out through the window, he might even have glimpsed the cause of Mohan Rao's demise in the distance. As it was, Chatpati was fully engaged trying to suppress his ire.

The ACP's PA, a matronly woman in khaki uniform sari, had instructed Chatpati on protocol as she led him in. Her eyes were kind.

"Don't forget to salute, Inspector. And best to wait to be asked a question before speaking." She smiled at him. "He's in a good mood today, so you should be fine. Just remember to salute!"

ACP Srinivasan had been first to speak, his greeting unexpectedly effusive.

"Ah! The hero of the hour! Come in, Inspector Chatpati."

Srinivasan had been lounging on his non-regulation sofa, his non-regulation shoes, glistening with someone else's spit and polish, resting on the non-regulation coffee table. The sofa was leather, the shoes brogues and the coffee table cut glass. Any one, Chatpati guessed, cost half a year's salary. The far wall, behind the ACP's desk, was tinted glass, fronted by a teak desk. The desk was flanked by the shields and flags of the Bangalore Police Service. The floor was polished granite, the air conditioned.

Srinivasan's attention had been on the huge flat-screen TV that dominated the near wall. Chatpati saluted and waited. Srinivasan glanced sidelong at him.

"Sit. Don't loiter," Srinivasan snapped, waving at a matching armchair.

Chatpati removed his hat and sat. Srinivasan had the physiognomy of a bon vivant; an improbably large nose overhung a caterpillar moustache and fleshy lips. His paunch cascaded over his Versace belt.

Srinivasan waved the remote control at the TV and turned the volume up.

"This will interest you," he said.

The Bangalore TV news was on. The screen showed a grizzled man in prison uniform and shackles being dragged out of a police van, surrounded by masked commandos wielding sub-machine guns. Chatpati recognised the High

Court in the background. Anchorwoman Nita Singh's stentorian delivery cut through the hubbub of journalists swarming about the prisoner.

"Today sees the beginning of the trial of Govind Prabhu, self-styled leader of the Kissan Yudh, the self-titled Farmer's War Party. Residents of Bangalore will remember it was not four months ago that the banned terrorist organisation launched their devastating chemical attack on the Vidhana Soudha[1]*. The terrorists claim they are fighting for the preservation of their traditional livelihoods against the incursion of foreign agro-tech companies. Six people died in the attack, including three school-children. It was only the prompt action of the police that prevented more casualties and saw the culprits swiftly brought to justice. The trial is expected to last several days, but the outcome is likely a foregone conclusion."*

The picture changed to a map of the city, shrouded in grey.

"And now, here's today's weather report. Smog in most areas-"

Srinivasan switched the TV off. "So," he said, smiling, "how does it feel to see justice done? Eh? To be the hero at the centre of the storm?"

Chatpati pursed his lips. "It's not something I think about. Sir."

Srinivasan sat up. "Really?" he sneered. " A commendation from the Justice Minister. A promotion. A cash reward from a grateful Government. Your face on the TV. And you don't think about it." Srinivasan shook his head in disbelief. "You are a very modest man, Inspector."

Chatpati shrugged. "I did not ask for the commendation. I refused the cash. And I avoided the media. As for the promotion-"

"You refused that too," Srinivasan said, nodding. "Strange man, Chatpati. Strange. Though," he wagged a finger, "some might say calculating. After all, what could possibly be more attractive than a hero? Except a *reluctant* hero? Eh?" Srinivasan leant over and slapped Chatpati on the shoulder. "Shabash! [2]Well done! Because, despite all your earnest refusals, you were rewarded. Am I wrong?"

Chatpati rubbed his shoulder. "I-"

"Oh yes," Srinivasan replied. "You refused the apartment, but you were forced into accepting it. The Minister can be very persuasive. Your wife was fed up of living in Police Quarters, no doubt. Nothing like air-conditioning, a fitted kitchen, a concierge, eh?And, instead of accepting the promotion to Assistant Commissioner of Police, you chose a sideways move. Heading the very first 'semi-autonomous police unit' in the City. Remind me what it's called again. Common Nonsense Unit, is it?"

Chatpati bristled. "Civil Nuisance Unit. Sir."

Srinivasan cackled, dispensing spittle. "Oh, yes. Civil Nuisance Unit. What a great name. You're at least half qualified to run that. You're not very civil, Inspector, but you're certainly a nuisance!"

Chatpati throttled his hat in his lap. "Again, sir-"

Srinivasan got to his feet and plodded over to his desk. "Yes, yes, not your choice. Victim of circumstance, blah, blah, blah. Spare me the details." He beckoned Chatpati over. "Come over here."

Behind the desk, Srinivasan looked even more the despot. Chatpati stood.

"Oh, for heaven's sake, sit, man," Srinivasan growled, flicking through papers. "Why such formality, eh? After all, we're all friends here. Now, where is that file?" He pressed a button on his phone.

"Yes, sir," the PA's voice said.

"Mina, where the bloody hell is that file? The German tourist? I thought I said to leave it on my desk."

"You did, sir," Mina replied. "But I had to update it with the medical report. Shall I bring it in?"

"Never mind," Srinivasan snapped. "You can give it to the Inspector when he leaves."

Chatpati felt a brief surge of hope. The end was in sight.

Srinivasan sat back in his chair and studied Chatpati.

"Some work for you, Inspector. To occupy you while your Unit is being set up. What is the status of your Nonsense Unit, by the way?"

"Nuisance. Sir." Chatpati replied. "The premises are being refurbished. We've recruited some staff, mostly volunteers from other divisions."

"I know about the volunteers," Srinivasan hissed, "since I'm paying their salaries for the next three months. Where is your premises? Remind me."

Chatpati swallowed. "The General Utilities building, sir. On Mahatma Gandhi Road. Top floor. The twenty-fourth."

Srinivasan scowled at him. "Utilities building? Not a police station?"

"No, sir. I thought it a better fit." And not subject to your routine interference, Chatpati did not say. "It's smack bang in the middle of our patch, the Central Business District. It's a government building, so it's rent free. It's mostly vacant, apart from a cinema on the ground floor, a vegetarian restaurant and a few small shops."

"What was on the top floor?" Srinivasan asked. "I can't recall."

"A nightclub. Sir."

Srinivasan's jaw dropped. "A nightclub?"

"Yes, sir," Chatpati replied, matter of fact. "It was repossessed. Two bars, a restaurant, an open-air balcony and lounge and a dance floor. And a mirrored disco ball." He paused. "Parquet, sir. The dance floor. You should drop by."

Chapter 3: Ill-met By Auto-Rickshaw

Inspector Chatpati emerged from the ACP's office around the middle of the morning. The sun was high in the sky. The traffic surged down Kasturba Road with a full-throated, asphyxiating roar. It was hot and getting hotter.

He waited for an auto-rickshaw[3] outside the gates, in the scant shade offered by an ancient cassia tree in bloom. The tree had stood here when the road had been laid during the British Raj[4]. It had outlasted the colonial conquerors; its roots had long since reclaimed most of the narrow, fractured pavement. Pedestrians picked their way past with care, avoiding loose flagstones that might send them tumbling into the mad throng of vehicles that raced past a shirtsleeve away.

The sting of ozone made Chatpati's nose run. He fished a face-mask out of his breast pocket and slipped it on. The smoke from the swarm of teetering buses, skittering auto-rickshaws and buzzing motorcycles gave the air a blue pall. The clamour of engines, horns, brakes and gears was deafening.

He soon realised that his chances of hailing an auto-rickshaw were small. It was peak time on one of the main arteries feeding Bangalore's buzzing heart. Factor in his being in police uniform and the probability of success approximated zero. Auto-rickshaws avoided policemen like the plague. Policemen rarely paid the fare.

Chatpati had waved at a couple of autos that puttered past but it was as if Chatpati were a low-caste Dalit[5] hailing an upper-caste Brahmin. The auto-drivers' gaze slipped right over him as if he didn't exist.

"Shall I stop one for you, Inspector?" the gate guard had asked. The guard had slipped the rifle off his shoulder and raised it across his chest. "This usually stops them."

"Good God, no!" Chatpati said, raising an arm. "Put that thing away! What's wrong with you?"

He had visions of an auto-rickshaw skidding to a halt before a pointed gun, only to be upended from behind by a speeding Municipal Corporation bus. Buses didn't stop for anything smaller than another bus. He could see the auto-rickshaw's tin-thin skeleton cleaved in two, passengers spilling out in a tangle of limbs, sarees spooling into spinning wheels, blood on the spokes and brains on the tarmac. He shuddered. He'd been at the scene of more road traffic accidents than he cared to remember.

The guard shrugged. "It works. Usually. Or I could call for a Hoysala[6]."

"No thanks," Chatpati said, "The driving is awful. I value my life. And it'll take an hour to arrive. They'll suddenly discover some urgent parking felony to prosecute instead."

"Try down the road, then, sir," the gate guard said, shouldering his rifle. "There are usually some auto-rickshaws outside Cubbon Park, near the Marriott, hustling for tourists." He gave Chatpati a conspiratorial grin. "You can sneak up on them. There will be at least one driver not in uniform."

The Municipal Corporation had recently mandated khaki uniforms for all auto-drivers. Compliance had been patchy, another rich source of revenue for the police.

Chatpati walked down Kasturba Road, sticking to the shade where he could. He made it halfway down when his luck changed. There, outside the entrance to the Industrial and Technology Museum, he happened across a gaggle of auto-rickshaws, parked carelessly by the pavement.

Three auto-drivers in various approximations of uniform surrounded a tall, moustachioed man in a dress shirt and tie. The tall man had placed a defensive blue fabric suitcase between him and the auto-drivers. They were so engrossed in heated discussion that none noticed Chatpati approach.

The tall man's voice rose above the din of traffic. He raised an arm, index finger pointed at the sky.

"I protest, thou recalcitrant vagabonds!" the tall man bellowed. "Thine attempts to inflict a calumny is treasonous!"

The two auto-drivers at either side of the third laughed outright. The third, clearly the leader, gave the suitcase a kick.

"Oy! Clown!" the leader growled, shaking a fist. "Stop talking nonsense and pay up. Don't try to cheat me! Pay the fare! Or else!"

The other two chipped in like a Greek chorus. "Yes. Pay up! Don't think you can cheat him just because he is an auto-driver! Better pay quick!"

The tall man drew himself up to his full height, towering above the drivers. ""Villains perpetually declaration themselves victim. Thine remonstrations fall on mute ears, vagrant! Dost thou not comprehend that I am a deputy of the justiciary!"

"What's going on here?" Chatpati said, in his official police voice. They turned to look at him. Shock registered on the faces of the auto-drivers, relief on that of the tall man. The two peripheral drivers began to edge away.

"Stop!" Chatpati said. "You two stay right there. You!"

He pointed at the leader, the one who had kicked the suitcase. "What's going on here? Why are you assaulting that suitcase?"

The fellow wilted, eyes to the ground. "It's nothing, sir," he mumbled. "Simple misunderstanding."

The tall man addressed Chatpati. "Penultimately! A fellow compatriot. Honourable compatriot, I entreat thee to imprison this multitude-"

Chatpati raised a hand. "You. Also stop." He stepped up to the ringleader and examined the regulation brass name plate pinned to the auto-driver's khaki uniform top. "Nagesh. That's your name, is it?" The man nodded, mute. "I asked you what's going on here. Speak up, damn it!"

Nagesh wrung his hands. "Sir, this fellow is refusing to pay his fare, sir. He began shouting! I – I felt threatened and-"

"Let me guess," Chatpati said, "you waved these two down to assist you. Am I correct?" He turned to the other two auto-drivers. They shrugged. "Assist? Or intimidate? Which is it?"

The auto-drivers stared at their feet and said nothing.

The tall man had been concentrating intently on the conversation. He spoke again to Chatpati. "Thou hast the great measure of the matter, respected compatriot of the justiciary. These vagabonds-"

Chatpati raised a hand. The tall man stopped. Chatpati addressed the auto-drivers. "Why does he speak like that?"

Nagesh shook his head and tapped his forehead. "Mad, sir. Unbalanced."

Chatpati's face was expressionless. "Where did you pick him up?"

"Majestic, sir."

Majestic was what the locals called the area around the

Majestic Theatre in the north of the city, in which the Central Bus and Train stations were located.

That made sense, Chatpati thought. The man was clearly from out of town. Chatpati looked him over. The traveller did not appear in the least intimidated. He had a trim moustache and well-maintained eyebrows. His nose was proud, his lips full. He was sweating freely in his long-sleeves and tie. There were damp patches under his arms.

"Where are you from?" Chatpati asked. The tall man looked puzzled. Chatpati tried again in the literary Kannada[7] the man had used. "What is thine abode, o compatriot?"

"Ah," the man smiled, "my native place is Cochin, that shining firmament in the fair kingdom of Kerala[8]."

Chatpati nodded. "Dost thou sojourn?

The man nodded. "Verily. I am arrived to engage in an enterprise of profession."

Chatpati's head was aching. He fished out his handkerchief and wiped his face. "Hast thou the faculty of other tongues?" he asked in hope. "English, mayhaps?"

"Why, yes," the tall man replied. In English. "I speak English. Of course. Why?"

"Thank God." Chatpati said. "Where did you learn to speak Kannada, may I ask?"

The tall man looked puzzled. "Well, from a book. It came with a CD-ROM."

Chatpati nodded. "I see. Was your Kannada book published any time in the last, say, twenty years?"

"I'm not sure. I got it from a second-hand bookshop. Why? What's wrong with my Kannada?"

"No one in Bangalore speaks like that," Chatpati said. "You're speaking the literary, declarative form of Kannada.

It's only ever used in traditional folk plays, like Yakshagana[9]."

The tall man looked nonplussed. "Oh. I-"

"Never mind," Chatpati said. "Let's stick to English. What's the problem here?"

"This fellow," the tall man said, pointing at the auto-driver Nagesh, "demanded five hundred rupees! For a fifteen minute journey! It's outrageous! I refused to pay! In Cochin, I would have had him arrested! I was about to ring for backup when you arrived."

"Cochin is Cochin. In Kerala State." Chatpati said. "This is Bangalore. In Karnataka State. Things are different here." The tall man bristled. "Nevertheless," Chatpati continued, "that fare is excessive. Wait a moment."

He turned to the auto-drivers and pointed at the two at the periphery. He used the guttural street Kannada of a true local. "You two! Bugger off. If I see your sorry arses again, you're in for a kicking. Get it? Now get lost."

The two men ran off towards their vehicles. Chatpati turned his attention to Nagesh. "As for you," he said, "this fellow says you demanded five hundred rupees."

"No sir!" Nagesh wailed. He folded himself into a crouch, hands raised overhead, palms together in the traditional gesture of supplication. "No sir! I just asked for a supplement over the standard fare because of rush hour and-"

"Idiot!" Chatpati cut him off. "Do you think I was born yesterday? There is no supplement for rush hour. Let's see what the fare on your meter is." Chatpati examined the fare meter on the remaining auto-rickshaw. The meter was off. Chatpati turned back. "Well, well, Nagesh. It looks like you didn't even turn the meter on. That's an automatic fine. Five hundred rupees. Get up, you idiot."

Nagesh struggled back upright and wrung his hands. ""Sir, please, sir. I don't have that much money. I just started my day. I have only two hundred sir. See, sir?" He produced a clutch of threadbare notes. "Please! If I don't make five hundred rupees today, I can't pay the daily rent for the auto. My family will—"

Chatpati rolled his eyes. "Oh, here we go. Your family will starve, your children will have to beg and your sainted dead mother will be refused entry to her heavenly abode. The usual excuses. Save it. Where were all your fine considerations when you summoned those two other idiots to intimidate this fellow, huh? And just around the corner from Assistant Commissioner's Office! Shameless! You should be fined just for being an idiot."

The tall man had had enough of being the observer. In English, he said "I demand you arrest this fellow. Such individuals deserve-"

"Never mind," Chatpati replied in English. "The matter is dealt with. For your information, the standard fare from Majestic to the city centre is fifty rupees. On this occasion, there's no charge. You are free to go. Goodbye."

Chatpati turned his back on the tall man and grabbed Nagesh by the collar. He thrust him towards his auto-rickshaw. "Get in. Start that thing up." Chatpati got in the rear passenger seat. "No fare for you for that trip, Nagesh. Serves you right. As for the fine, you can either pay it or you can take me to MG Road. Which is it to be?"

Nagesh cranked the machine to life. He turned back to Chatpati, hands folded. "Please, sir. I would be honoured to take you wherever you wish."

The tall man had picked up his suitcase. Chatpati called out to him as the auto-rickshaw pulled away.

"Have a pleasant stay in Bangalore. And buy another Kannada textbook!"

Did you spot the reappearance of Sub-Inspector Nair?

If you would like to read more, The Tender Coconut Tamasha is available in ebook and paperback.

Follow the link below to find it on your preferred platform.

BOOKS 2 READ

www.books2read.com/tendercoconut

Lightning Source UK Ltd.
Milton Keynes UK
UKHW021127211222
414263UK00017B/1118